CORNERED BY THE DEADLY LEERIS

A bale had been prised out and not replaced. Jerrod Northi began to wriggle into the space it had left, crouching. In caution and in haste, which turned to horror as he saw a flash of light and heard the thud of another and then another and then another leeri. One hit a projecting bale and fell, thrashing, to the floor. Another fell from above, like a caterpillar from a tree, landed on the protruding edge of a hide halfway between niche and floor, and then began to make its way inexorably upwards . . . inching, sometimes, like a worm . . . writhing, sometimes, like a serpent . . . crawling, sometimes, like a lizard . . . slowly, for the most part . . . but, slowly or otherwise, shining, shining its cold and its hunger, upward. Always upward.

And then it sprang. . . .

The Enemy of My Enemy

AVRAM DAVIDSON

A BERKLEY MEDALLION BOOK
Published by
BERKLEY PUBLISHING CORPORATION

COPYRIGHT © 1966 BY AVRAM DAVIDSON

Published by arrangement with
the author's agent

BERKLEY MEDALLION EDITION, DECEMBER, 1966

BERKLEY MEDALLION BOOKS *are published by*
Berkley Publishing Corporation
15 East 26th Street, New York, N. Y. 10010

BERKLEY MEDALLION BOOKS ® TM 757,375

Printed in the United States of America

CHAPTER ONE

It was the Hour of the Dog, midway between midnight and dawn, and even in swarming, pullulating Pemath Old Port, things were quiet. That is, they were as quiet as they ever got. Somewhere not very far off a harlot tirelessly tinkled her bronzes in hopes of attracting a customer. The thick, evil smell of *par*tripes frying in old oil advertised at least one all night cook-stall was still open for business. The incessant *thud thud thud* of staff upon stone warned of a patrolling old watchman. Someone sang mad nonsense in a high, thin voice; voice, as it broke off into an unmistakable retching cough, giving notice that the *kip* dens were still open despite all the pious support given the Suppression Campaign by the junta of civil and military thieves making up the current Pemath government. A dull, dancing glow from the walled-off Ruins, and the sound of noisemakers, advertised to any who cared that a party was in progress . . . some would call it a kiddy fair . . . some, blunter, a child hunt . . . but not many would bother to call it anything. Consciences were not tender in Pemath. And, periodically, from the north, the boom and light flash of some dirty old freighter announced cargoes bound for Tarnis, Lermencas, Baho, or other on-world ports. The beggar cripple asleep in his kennel on the corner did not stir. Exceptions here made no rule: Old Port, still, was —for Old Port—still.

The building which gave niche-space to the beggar as indifferently as a tree might lodge a bird was typical Old Port construction: massy, filthy, ancient, indestructible, its huge halls and lobbies, relics of a more prosperous age, long since divided and subdivided into small and smaller rooms. Only in front of the elevator did more space remain unfilled. There was no immediate reply from it, and the man waiting pressed the signal panel impatiently two or three more times. After a while the slight sounds of machinery moving within the shaft appeased his annoyance a bit, but the panel remained dark. Broken, probably, and likely to remain so forever more. Presently, the cage set down and a tiny, withered hand thrust out through the hole in front; he dropped a coin into it; the hand withdrew; the door slid open.

It was an old granny of a lift-woman, huddled on the stool beside the control board. The rest of the family lay snoring behind the screen along one side. There was room enough. It was long since the large hydraulic elevator had carried the bulk freights it had been designed for. A faint wail came from a little box on struts; the granny immediately reached out a bare and dirty foot, gave it a swing. The baby gave a tiny grunt, subsided. An early breakfast had already been started, steamed thinly on the small stove. It was entirely possible the baby had never left the lift since it was born, might never leave it for years. "Twenty-three," the passenger said.

Granny shook her wrinkled apple of a head, started the cage up. "Twenny-tree, not stop," she said. "Stop twenny, you go-walk sout-side, go-take local a twenny-tree."

The man wrinkled his face at the smells, shook his head. "Stop at twenty-five," he said. "I'll walk down."

"Affa midnight, cos' a ticky," the granny said. He gave his head a slight shake, repeated, firmly: Twenty-five. The granny did not bother to shrug. The gambit almost never worked, but she tried it every time nonetheless. Why not? Words were free, and a ticky was not to be despised. Three of them bought a mouth piece of bread.

The dim cage slid up its spoke. Once, through a much patched but still (or again) broken part of the rear cage, the man saw the weary and slack-mouthed and besmeared face of a greasy who had crawled into her tween-floor's hideyhole as the cage passed by. Maintenance was evidently not being totally neglected. Brief wonder what price the lift operators farmed the concession for passed through the passenger's mind. No use to ask. Pemathi didn't incline to give out that kind of information. If the granny were to tell and her tax to be increased seven years later, she'd remember and blame it on that. Odd patterns of light and sound filtered in as they swam up the elevator shaft. At floor eleven the faint green glimmer conveyed to his eyes the same message as the yammering and coughing of the *kip* heads there did to his ears. Floor fifteen, the discordant and assonant hymnody of a back-country cult conventicle. Floor seventeen blazed with light and echoed with the *chick chick* chatter of a 3D camera making porno shots. From the far, or south, side of floor twenty a man's voice echoed in bursts of insane staccato rage, while a woman screamed shrilly and without pause. The other floors were all dim and still.

At twenty-five he got out and walked towards the stairs. The elevator door slid shut and the whole works—snores, smells, screens, granny, baby, breakfast, sustenance and slavery—sank from sight. The grimy walls were thick with signs and diagrams advertising an infinity of commodities and services and showing how to get there from here. The man paused to read, passed on, got lost, retraced his steps, went nowhere near the stairs, and finally opened, then closed behind him the translucent shutter of a three-dish diner. A limp-looking, gray-faced waiter lurched up from the bench where he'd been lying, made a wide-sweeping, weary gesture. "You go-sit any down you like," he muttered. Cleared his throat, spat tidily under the bench.

The man sat with a grunt and a glance at the shutter he'd just come through. "What's three for tonight?" he asked.

"Tonight tree, go-eat roas' *par* leg, hot soup, sweety bowl."

"Mm. Might have *par*. No leg, though. How about head? Stuffed." The waiter started to shake his head. "With old-fashioned green sauce," the man added. "South Coast style. You know."

The waiter bowed his head instead, considered, with his lip stuck out for a second. "I go-as' cook." He started away, his feet going *plop plop,* old waiters' feet, like they had no bones in them. Turned his head, slowed down: "How you go-like sauce? Smoot?"

" 'Smooth?' No no. Sharp as it comes."

Plop plop. The limp figure vanished away into the shadows at the back. The customer glanced around. Obviously an old, *old* established three-dish place—and never been painted or decorated—no attempt to attract the foreign or nouveau riche trade, or even the bright coins some swaggering shop-boy had abstracted from the till to lavish in hopes of impressing his first whore. The customers' tickys went nowhere but into the contents of the big, the little, and the middle-sized bowl which constituted the traditional and staple Pemathi meal. And the customers would be those and only those who lived or worked on or visited the twenty-fifth floor for business or pleasure in its eighth of a mile of rabbit-warren rooms and halls: they either ate the daily three or they went without or went elsewhere. It was reasonable to assume they ate.

Pemathi were realists—all the swarming, corrupt, charming, brutal, tolerant, indifferent, cruel scores of millions of them. Indeed, it was their own proverb which had it that *The Ocean-Serpent engirdles the whole world . . . but its fundament lies in Pemath.*

And still the waiter didn't come back and then he did and paused to rest his poor flattened old feet. "You go-come a cook."

The customer nodded and got up and walked across the pitted floor. The waiter's eye rolled just a bit. The man stopped short. The waiter's eye rolled away. He made a slight, jerky motion—as if involuntarily. The customer seemed in one second to rise from the floor and hurtle through the air —the waiter gave a frightened gasp, and was gone—the other landed, spun around, and was out past the shutter before it shattered into smoking shards.

* * *

His pursuers would hardly want to set the whole floor on fire, though, and he knew this and counted on it, too. He could smell the charge, feel his back tingling. It would hurt, horribly, later. But if he stood still to reflect on this, there would be no later. His eye lit on the symbol for a two-ticky public pissoir, and he had dodged inside the half-folded shutter in a second. The gaffer huddled in his corner half-looked up from sleep, a coin fell in his lap, he engulfed it, grunted, returned at once to his frowsty old dreams, neither noticing nor caring that his customer flitted out the other door without pausing to use bowl or booth.

Rapidly, the fleeing man tried to orient himself. The elevator—the one he'd come up on—was back *that* way—the other one, the local, and the stairs, were over *that* way: south. Then *this* way, the way ahead of him, was . . .

Something came hissing through the air, hit the wall just above and before him, bounced off, and . . . The man danced madly, his hands and feet flying, dodging, dodging, all the while trying to get by and past the looping, twisting, thrashing band of light which jerked and flung itself about and about, always coming nearer and nearer to him along the floor like some insane serpent; insane, nonetheless purposeful: a leeri, created in the instant of its expulsion from the small tank-gun in the hands of who? behind, there. A half-life thing, and that life low and primitive, the outer

layer calorotropic, desperately and forever seeking warmth
... any warmth ... that of the human body, for example; the
inner layer almost pure energy. If the leeri were to reach his
ankles, it would instantly wind round them like a moebius
strip, trip him, bring him down, cutting deeper and deeper
into his flesh.

And if his neck—?

He dodged, he danced, he got by, he ran, lightly and on his
toes, arms out for balance. For this while along that aisle he
was safe, for the leeri, that while longer which it lived, barred
the way behind him, like the other edge of the sword.

He turned off into another alleyway; still keeping his destination in mind, he thought now to reach it via knight's
rather than rook's move. If he could. He heard nothing but
the *pad pad* of his feet in their thin-hide shoes. Doubtless
those behind him could take him in quick enough time if
they sounded an alarm. And, doubtless, they had their reasons for sounding none. The air in here was thicker than
ever, and in a second he saw the source, bale after bale of
badly-cured *ort* hides, salt crystals oozing out between the
layers. Some leather merchant had his lair hereabouts; the
man squeezed by the packs of skins; something squeezed by
the man—who hissed in his breath, pressed himself against
the bales. Then let out his breath. A rat. Fortunately not a
hungry rat or a fierce rat, just a rat. A soon-vanished rat. His
eyes went towards the direction he'd been fleeing. He cocked
his head, listened. Winced. And at once began to climb the
pile of packs of skins.

Fortunately for him, it had not been piled snugly. Here, a
bale was loose enough for foothold but not, thank the stars!
loose enough to fall and give him away. And here, luckier
yet, a bale had been prised out ... and not replaced. He
began to wriggle into the space it had left, crouching, sideways and backwards. In caution and in haste, which turned
to horror as he saw a flash of light and heard the thud of
another and then another and then another leeri. One hit a
projecting bale and fell, thrashing to the floor. Another rebounded from the opposite wall, and joined its writhing fellow. But the third fell from above, like a caterpillar from a
tree, landed on the protruding edge of a hide halfway between niche and floor, and then began to make its way inexorably upwards ... inching, sometimes, like a worm ...
writhing, sometimes, like a serpent ... crawling, sometimes,
like a lizard ... slowly, for the most part ... but, slowly or

otherwise, shining, shining its cold and its hunger, upwards. Always upward.

And then it sprang.

The rat squeaked once, shrill, fearful.

The sounds which had been off there in the dimness back along the hall came advancing. Before: hesitant. Cautious. Now: certain. Confident. Man stooped, shoulders hunched, only a section of face revealed, brow and eye and upper cheek. Almost a moan, then, dismayed disappointment at the sight of the three leeri wrapped around the dying rat. But not for long. Half-cured leather, hard as boards, a whole pack of it crashed down upon him, flung him to the filthy floor. For a slow second his visible hand seemed to stroke the floor, softly, tenderly, lovingly. Then it lay still.

* * *

Atén aDuc pursed out his mouth and squeezed it up so that his thin, red Pemathi moustache was pressed up close to his broad and thick Pemathi nose.

"No, who go-chase you wit leeri?" he asked.

His guest, who had told his story sitting nervously or jumping to his feet in fits and starts, once more composed his long and slim body onto the cushioned up-seat and angrily squinted his eyes. "Oh, jape that chopchop talk, 'Ten!" he said. "You can speak properly, better than I. . . ." His back had been dressed, he felt no more actual pain.

Atén aDuc shrugged, sighed. "True, true, Jer. But my opportunities for doing so are so exceedingly limited. For the most part, were I to do so, those who cannot would be humiliated, and those who can would be annoyed. Pemathi are supposed to speak chopchop to foreigners. It's one of the rules of the game. For one thing, if Pemathi speak foreign languages well, then the implication is that foreigners ought to speak Pemathi well. Which, of course, is quite true. Still. . . . I have heard of cases where foreigners who met in other countries—and for that matter, on other worlds—found themselves obliged to speak chopchop because it was the only tongue they had in common. Perhaps we should urge its adoption in place of InterGal. Eh, Jer? But we avoid the harsh answer, like an *ekl* sucking eggs. *Who*?"

The room was hung on all its walls from floor to ceiling in those classical Pemathi rug-tapestries which are no longer being woven: red to red-brown to brown were these, at least a hundred shades of each, presenting no discernible pattern or motif at all to the direct glance; then falling into pleasant hints of things around the periphery of vision once one looked away. In the center of the triangle formed by the three long up-seats stood the miniature pavilion of burnished copper which served as cook stove, foot warmer, incense burner, water heater, and so on. In the hollow atop the very center rested a three-quarter-globe bowl from which protruded a jeweled drinking tube, the filigreed bulb at its end protecting the drinker from the pleasantly tart but acid textured pulp of the fruit within. The room was just the sort of place that touring visitors of Pemath always wanted much to see but almost never did see; it was classically Pemathi . . . at least until you noticed that the carven cask-wood ark in the north corner contained a 3D viewer instead of ancestral effigies, or that Atén aDuc under his long embroidered tunic —the loops and frogs of which, contrary to all etiquette, were left unfastened—wore the kind of waistcoat which Tarnisi women used to affect for winter sports. . . . Things like that.

"Eh, Jerred? *Who* was chasing you with leeri? Any idea? You—"

"—must have some? Sure I have. The trouble is, I've got too many. I haven't exactly been a nice boy, let's confess it. How many cargoes I've cracked and stolen down Portside— I don't know. You ought to, you bought half of them. Multiply by two. . . ."

Atén aDuc pulled his head back and thrust his chin out in the typical Pemathi posture of mild protest. "My dear Northi, but who could possibly resent that? '*Stolen*'? Nonsense. 'Diverted' is by far the better word. If the average shipper gets through four cargoes out of five and doesn't lose more than a quarter of the ones he does get through, why, he's delighted, my boy, delighted! That's not a thing to be called theft, that's normal commercial attrition. Why, if a commodity persists in going through untouched time after time, the agents' feelings are hurt. They feel a reflection has been cast upon its value. No, no, nobody is going to chase you with leeri for *that*. And, besides, that was years ago. No. . . ."

"I took Otár oDon's women away from him. Both of them. *You* remember. He and his group swore—"

His host rose, yawning, tapping his nose emphatically. "No, no. Otár oDon's too busy drinking himself to death to bother, and his company has scattered from the back country to the South Coast; besides, really. A fire-charge, just possibly a group type of thing. Just possibly. Knife, club, rope, much more their style of thing. But—leeri? *Pushipushi.* Absurd."

Jerred Northi grimaced, tugged at his drink. "No, you're probably right. There are maybe one or two outfits on World Orinel less likely to come leeri-spitting . . . but I wouldn't know them. Well. The same objection to 'Tar's being behind it applies just as well to most of the other people whose toes I've stepped on. And, also: 'that was years ago.' So. What's left? What's happened lately? Tow-tapping. I suppose I've tapped more tows these past two years than anyone else." His frown lifted a trifle. "And tapped them clean, too. I hate a messy tapping. Waste. Just waste."

Not the least of the dreadful ironies of overpopulated Pemath, where most people hungered, was that it actually exported edibles. The underfed mass of Pemathi dressed their scanty victuals with the rank, thick oil of the *oron*-nut, produced in the vast plantations of the Lermencasi-owned archipelago of Ran—not because they preferred it, but because they could afford no better. The bulk of Pemathi-produced *ty*-seed oil, the delicate and savory *tya*, went overseas to Lermencas, Baho, Tarnis, and all the other, richer lands of Planet Orinel. The peasants who picked it, the toilers who pressed it, were forbidden so much as to lick their fingers of it, lest they form the habit of dipping those fingers into it, thus diminishing the amount by a few tickys' worth per thousand. Oils and syrups and similar commodities arrived and departed in huge subsurface tankers of foreign registry at Pemath New Port, governed by the Joint Commission on which the Pemathi representation was but the echo to the Interleague members, and patrolled by the Commission's crack police.

But the cargoes were made up for overseas shipment, or broken up for internal distribution, in Pemath Old Port. Which was something else again. The dirty, slow, powerful paratugs, obsolete elsewhere for years, still plied their ways through the oily, shallow waters of the Inner Sea, north and south of the Double Ports, towing behind them their liqueous cargo in great, fish-shaped tows of tough but flexible plastoid, which ran more below the water than above it. A skilled "tow-tapper," as these latter-day pirates were called, adjusting his paravanes to a nicety, could sweep down of a dark night, cut the tow loose, and carry it away behind his own—fleeter, armed—vessel, without losing a drop of it. Sometimes a firm of tow-shippers was informed that "a loose tow had been found adrift"—or, "washed ashore"—and those whose prize it was by right of salvage would sell it back at a reasonable price. But often as not no open traces were ever observed again. Owners' names could not be stamped upon a liquid. The trade, or profession, was a risky one; it usually paid off well, though.

Crime, however, is rarely sterile, and organized crime never is. Infection breeds infection; officials who wink at one class of offenses soon become stone-blind to others. Some who become aware do not always abhor, and very often they envy, and very often they emulate. Behind the lion (so ran a proverb of Ancient Earth: proverb no more than a statement of fact) followed the hyena, and behind the hyena, the jackal. In Pemath a man who merely deprived another man of property suffered little stigma—unless, of course, he should be caught and punished—he paid, instead, in keeping corrupt officials and in risking and often suffering the depredatory attacks of those whose policy was to do unto others what those others had done unto others yet. Big thieves have little thieves to bite 'em. And bought officials demonstrate their corroded morality by often not staying bought. Tow-tappers, however neatly and cleanly they tapped their tows, had to fight off the human hyenas and jackals who snarled and yelped and snapped for a bite of the carcass...

And those who had owned the carcass while it was still a live thing, however used to the circumstances of Pemathi commerce and Pemathi crime they might be, did not necessarily always shrug philosophically and obey the great eternal commercial adage, *Pass it along to the consumer*.

"Oh, come," Atén aDuc said, disparagingly, lifting the lid off a section of the bright copper complex, and fishing out a goody which he popped into his mouth; chewed; swallowed; brushed scented water across his lips and wiped them dry. Continued, "Surely you don't believe that the Joint Commission or the Interleague Powers hired a man to sling leeri at you?"

Jerred Northi stretched out in his up-seat and looked at the carven ceiling. "Not directly, no. But it's the IL nations who've been clamoring for a crackdown on piracy, as they're pleased to call it. 'Wherever it may be found'—a pretty piece of funny talk; where *is* it found? Only here. And the Joint Commission is their local arm and hand. So the JC puts the screws on its Pemathi members until they can't get by with smiles and lies and promises. Well, 'Ten . . . What do you suppose? Your government, or what passes for it, may be resigned, if it has to, to going without the graft that towtapping means—for a while. But they're not for a while or a minute going to risk an actual investigation. Are they? Why should they trust *me*? I don't trust *them*. Why shouldn't Governancer uFon or Militar iGer or the rest of them want me out of the way? Think how embarrassing for them if I were got into the interrogation seat and made to answer questions about whom I bribed and with how much or how often? Your governancers and militars would think no more of leeri-ing me than of cracking a flea."

Atén aDuc sucked a last shred of savor from his teeth. "Or of breaking a butterfly on a wheel, since we seem to be drawing metaphors from the insect world. As far as scruple was concerned. But the effort rules it out. No. I am not convinced."

Neither was his younger guest. Still, he had no other notions. Once again he went through the night's events, beginning with the even earlier events—the crackdown on towtapping, the raid on the little South Coast harbor where he'd set up headquarters over two years ago, the sequestration of his account in the National Fiscal, the appearance of Pemathi police and militia in three successive places he passed through on his flight north—which, he was convinced, had served somehow as a prelude. "I wasn't fool enough to keep very much . . . comparatively . . . in the NatFisc, of course. I've got quite a bit, well, some place else. Not that I mistrust you, you understand. That wasn't what I went to New Port for, though. And I really had thought that no one there connected me—me, I mean, the tow-tapper, with the me who'd been keeping up my old apartments there. So it was rather a chill to spot the JC's plaindressmen keeping watch outside. That indefinable, unmistakable look they have, you know—

"Well, that stamped it and sealed it, as far as I was concerned. I've been in Pemath most of my life, and despite all my bitching and slanging, I'm used to it and hadn't planned on quitting it. Not so soon as this, anyway. But what else is there to do? Obviously I can't leave by any of the open ways. Not now. So I went up to Matán iNac's threedish place to make the other kind of connection. Said the right words, everything. And they—he—whoever—was ready and waiting for me. First the fire-charge, then the leeri. So: if it's not your chiefs of state, then who in the Hell is it?"

Atén aDuc picked up from the little stand beside him a

thular, long, and dark of wood, and rich with inlays and bandings of silver and gold, and blew a rift of soft, deep notes from it. Only a fragment of music, brief, but it evoked faint conjectures of the time when Pemath and her people were not divided between the oppressing few and the oppressed many. With an abrupt gesture quite different from his usual mannered calm, he put the instrument back on its elaborately carven stand, turned his full attention to his younger friend once more.

"The time to reflect on that and on other matters of philosophical inquiry will be when you are far away and safe. You ought to have realized that Matán iNac can operate only with someone's—quite a few someones'—connivance. As it happens, that particular graft is one of the plums of two of my fellowcountrymen whose names you mentioned just a little while ago: Governancer uFon and Militar iGer. They *could* have wanted you out of the way: true. They *could* have figured that sooner or later you would wind up at 'Tan's: true. They *could* have had a man waiting to fire-charge you: true. But . . . they could have the same man—or another— waiting to leeri you? *Not* true. Leeri are too new, and if one thing is sure it is that Pemath does not try new things. That is why we are what we are and how we are. Psychologically, I tell you, it is impossible that what passes for our government should have tried that. And it seems to me equally impossible, psychologically, that anyone who would try leeri would have first tried an attack with anything as oldfashioned and clumsy as a fire-charge. So—well—add it up. What do you get?"

Jerred said, promptly, "I get the message that I better get out of here and far away from here, and quietly, and quickly. Because, although I don't know who or why, someone (or, as you'd put it) a few someones besides the government of Pemath is after my ass. You know almost everything. Do you know who?"

Atén aDuc shook his head, pulled at his lower lip. "No. I repeat, that's not the prime question. Better ask: *where* is it you're going that's far away from here? And *how* are you going to do it quietly and quickly? I don't know those answers, either. I know who does, though . . . for a price of course . . . need I say? . . . in Pemath? . . . for a price . . . . Lady Mani."

The younger man made a small sound of surprise, quickly overcome by a long sound of disgust.

15

"But why?" aDuc was himself surprised at this reaction.

A look of loathing, hatred, contempt, of even physical revulsion, writhed upon Jerred Northi's face.

"There's a why," he said, after a moment, "and there's a why not. It's not because she was certainly once a whore, though she's pretty much covered that up. And it's not because she's certainly still herself a whoremonger, though she pretty much covers *that* up. I have no right to despise the shopkeeper where I've gone myself to shop. But—damn it, 'Ten! She runs the biggest kiddy fair cartel in the country. Doesn't she? I mean—*child hunts!*"

The older man sighed. "You haven't lived in Pemath long enough, Jer," he said, "no matter how long you have lived here, if you still react like that. Pemath is not Tarnis. Or Baho or Lermencas. Or anywhere else. Do you know how many of our children die of hunger alone every day? You say, 'Oh, how dreadful that this child should be hunted!' *I* say, 'The day the child is hunted is the day it's sure to eat.' Don't bother me with your tender stomach. *Pushipushi.* What, you are *still* making faces? By my forefathers' foreskins! *Why?*"

"Because," said Northi, in a low voice that commanded attention better than a shout. "Because . . . I think . . . that I was once, myself . . . I'm not sure, I'm not sure, but I'm sure enough . . . that I was at least one time a huntee-kid myself —" He looked sick. He seemed to crouch, and he swallowed hard.

Atén aDuc's face for a moment showed shock, then sympathy. Then simply fatigue. Then all three vanished. The urbane mask slid into place again. He shrugged. "Well, there you are. And you are alive and almost thirty years old and coarsely healthy and you have had much sport and pleasure in your life and you hope to grow much older and stay at least as healthy and have much *more* sport and pleasure. So you will allow me to gamble on the likelihood that you were not followed here, and to introduce you to the presence of Lady Mani—not so simple or easy, you know—and allow her to take it (and you) from there. Or perhaps you prefer to go on dodging around until someone sets you on fire or loops a leeri around your neck. Eh?"

"No. . . ."

Atén aDuc stroked his thin, red moustache. He gave a very small, very short sigh. Then he reached over for his *thular* once again. "By and by I shall set things in motion. It's still too early. Meanwhile, there is food, there is drink, there are things to inhale, there is also some music about to be played. Or you may simply wish to sleep."

He placed the *thular* to his lips. The notes came forth, slow, simple at first, then less slow and more intricate. His face changed utterly. It became the face of a lover, lost in the contemplation of his love.

Jerred Northi crouched on the up-seat.

CHAPTER TWO

Ronk Krakar, a typical Bahon (so he thought of himself and was content to have others think of him) with a typically explosive Bahon name, was feeling altogether rather explosive. It wasn't that the Tarnisi were unpleasant to him. At least, certainly not unpleasant in a way he'd met with elsewhere, because he was a Bahon . . . the way some other nationals were unpleasant because the United Syndicates of Bahon had a deserved reputation for staunchly looking out for their own interests. There had never been any disgusting incident of going to the Tarnisi theater and being obliged to walk out in the middle of a so-called comedy because the thing contained actors made up as caricatures of Bahon. That had happened to him before; he grunted angrily as he recalled his then-host following him out with feigned regret which broke into uncontrolled laughter as he recalled the stage mockery he was even then deploring: mock Bahon names, mock Bahon accents. No—

There was nothing coarse about the Tarnisi. And they had no particular prejudice against Baho or the Bahon. It was simply that they were concerned only with themselves, and seemed unable ever to regard foreigners as fellow adults. Here, for example: He'd been waiting many minutes in the guest rooms of the office in Tarnis Town of their current Commercial Deputy, Hob Mothiosant. For a man not to be prompt for an appointment was bad enough, for a businessman it ought to have been out of the question, but for a government official . . . ! And then this effete nonsense of "guest rooms" as office adjuncts! Krakar had come on business, important business, traveling thousands of miles, and not to be shown into some sort of—he lacked the words, the experience—was brusque to the pretty girl who was opening boxes of games (*games!*) and offering to show him how they were played and to play with him (*play!*)—or to dance with him or for him, or to employ various musical instruments in his entertainment. No, he did not desire that, nor did he wish to swim or to bathe . . . his mind, not too accomplished in the language, backtracked, corrected itself, was scandalized: She had offered to bathe him! How effete, how typical!

He cleared his throat, glanced around the (admittedly) gracious chambers, resisted an angry impulse to stride out, flung himself down in a chair and picked up a book without looking at it. In an instant the guest-girl, not ruffled in the slightest, was at his side, turning the pages for him.

"See, this is a very ancient illustrated text, my great lord," she said, in her pleasant voice, "of our national epic, *The Volanthani*. Lord Maddary rides home from the hunting and finds his wife has been rapted away by the Volanth. . . ." Her slender hands turned the page, rings flashing on long, lovely fingers. Tarnisi in archaic costume made stylized gestures, were attacked by a multitude of ugly, stunted, apelike figures, caricatures, uniformly evil of expression. "See, my great lord: the Volanth. Ugh, how disgusting!" Gradually Krakar allowed the pleasure of voice and presence to soothe him of his annoyance, took no particular notice of the narrative except to derive mild, automatic, low-keyed pleasure from the soft colors of the pictures. Was, at length, caught up with some confusion and surprise at the end.

"I don't understand. I thought she was his wife."

"She was his wife, great lord."

"Then why did he kill her?"

"She could not have returned to live with him, great lord, after the disgrace of being held in capture by the Volanth."

"I see. . . ." But did he? "Well. In that case, since he could not keep her, why did he bother to go after her in the first place?"

The girl seemed at some loss to know what to answer. Probably no one had ever brought this inconsistence to her attention before. Chimes sounded. She rose from her knees, gently closed the book. "Pemathi boy is coming presently, my great lord."

The "boy" turned out to be a portly, elderly Pemathi, grey shot all through his once red hair, and dressed in a fashion which he, Krakar, had never observed in Pemath—or, indeed, anywhere else outside of books. Drab kilt and coat and cap, unknown in Pemath proper for generations, were evidently still not merely traditional, but required, here among the sojourning Pemathi servant class in Tarnis.

"Master, we go-see Himself now. Sorry for bad delay. My own guilt."

Ronk Krakar did not believe it for a moment, of course, but at least the excuse returned him to a familiarity where tardiness was at least a matter incurring guilt and requiring excuses. Behind him he heard the guest-girl murmur, "Return another time, my great lord, and renew my joy." He grew a trifle warm about the skin, reflecting on the phrase, and its possible (though this time unjustified) implications. If someone had told him that the offices of the Commercial Deputation were the suites of a palace, Krakar would not have had any trouble believing it. Astonishing! How could so impractical a people have amassed such richness? The nuances of the beauty might be open to discussion, subject to opinion; the richness, never.

Mothiosant greeted him with some politely subdued murmur of a phrase which might have meant, My cousin's uncle, or, My uncle's cousin . . . not so near a degree of kinship which would have required them to kiss, not so distant a one which might have offended. Assuming Krakar to be susceptible to offenses of that sort. Tardiness as a matter of offense evidently did not cleave to the Tarnisi Commercial Delegate's mind.

"I have been painting leaves again," the man said, gesturing to a complex of art supplies which should have been sufficient to paint an entire forest. The gesturing hand came to rest in mid-air, fingers limp and languid before a sheet of some dark substance on which was a darker smudge. "You do not care for it," he said, after a moment's polite uncomprehending silence. "You are correct not to. What says Sohalion? and, after all, Sohalion *is* leaves: if Sohalion has not said something on the subject, let no one now venture to bother saying it. 'One should begin to paint leaves at the age of ten, one should continue painting leaves for another thirty years; after that, one may have arrived at the possibility of knowing how to paint leaves.' Well—" He lifted his hand, his face, his eyebrows. "And I have done none of these things. Of course it is but a wretched daub, tear it up, destroy it, Arád iGen."

"I go-do so, Yourself," the aid said, obediently.

Krakar ventured to turn the talk onto the proper track. "Sir, the purchasing contracts for the resins—"

"Ah, why speak of the dull past?" Mothiosant arose from the contoured bench. "We have a pleasant, I must hope, a fascinating, I must hope, section of the present to enjoy. What says Alanas? 'The present is a cross section of eternity,' is it not so? Yellowtrees, have you never been there? You will enjoy, I must hope, your visit. I know that I and all of us will enjoy your visit. So. Give me your august sleeve, and I will, as we leave, point out to you one or two or at most three things of worth (some would say, 'beauty'; such presumption is not for me) which do not disgrace this building, sordid function though it serves."

He took hold of the tiniest bit of Ronk Krakar's sleeve with his thumb and forefinger. The Bahon's eyes, bewildered, met those of the Pemathi, who said, "Before, we go-take Master clotes and oter tings, go-pack tem good. Master needn' go-worry. Go-have nice visit on Yellowtrees, Himself's estate."

Urged forward by the most infinitesimal of physical pressures, yet able no more to resist than if drawn by titan engines, Krakar could not on the other hand completely surrender his proper purpose. "Sir," he said, firmly, as they walked through the corridor; "Sir, concerning the purchasing contracts for the resins—"

His guide turned to him a look both humorous and rueful. "Ah, still the past, my kinsman's kin? Was not the resin satisfactory?" Face, with an effort, turned grave. " 'Rad, discern from the records those responsible for poor resins, we shall have them flogged . . . or something unpleasant. You," he said to the Bahon, "will be content."

"I do not—Sir, I—"

A slight sigh escaped Mothiosant. He paused in front of a cabinet containing something which glistened. "Three years ago, I must hope I am correct, your august nation purchased resins, did they not so? Ah, you see," he smiled, faintly, "you say that we Tarnisi have no head for business, but I am sure my memory does not fail me here, I must— Arád iGen! Did not three years ago Baho-men buy resin-chop?"

"They go-do so, yes, Yourself, before tree year."

The Tarnisi smiled blandly. Ronk made a considerable effort and smiled back. "It is true, sir. Three years ago, two years ago, and one year ago, we bought resins from Tarnis.

They were quite satisfactory. We bought them seven years ago, eight years ago, eleven years ago, and so on. We buy them every year, sir. Every year that we can."

Mothiosant's smile had not ebbed during this flow of statistics, it had merely frozen. "Is it so, then. How unforgivably stupid of me. I should be flogged. Well, then, this year you shall buy them cheaper, but let us not discuss it now. Afterwards, kin Krakar, you and 'Rad will arrange the matter."

The Bahon's fingers twitched on the portfolio containing the contracts. Again his eyes met the Pemathi's. The latter's gaze was now as bland as his own master's smile, as stylized as the intricate carvings in this so-called Hall of Commerce. "Ah, Yourself, too bad. Resins no come up from sout. Trees all sick tis year. We go-get resins, Volant in sout all hunger, you-know. No resin-chop for go-sell. Ah—"

The Deputy dropped the whole matter instantly with, "There you are. Alas. Now, my august kith, do you see the grain of this inscription tablet of the Eleventh Cycle? Is it not beautiful?"

His "august kith" swallowed something stiff and bristly in his throat. He knew what this meant. Well, better to have found it out before the office at home had made commitments. More than once, in fact quite often, contracts for the purchase of commodities had been made with Tarnis, only to have them casually broken because the latter had simply not bothered to look before they signed. It would be beneath them to engage in commerce efficiently, to gauge their resources' futures before committing them. No resins! Well . . . once more, briefly, he met iGen's eye. Yes, yes. He knew well enough what it meant. The Pemathi would have known quite, quite early in the season that the crop was going to fail. And doubtless he had scrounged around, bought up what there was to buy on his own and secret account; now one would have to do business with *him* . . . at high prices . . . plus bribery . . . The man bowed slightly. His capped head was immaculate. In a way, Krakar reflected, irritation already giving way to resignation, in a way it was too bad that one could not simply do business all of the time with the local Pemathi, and leave their Tarnisi masters quite alone to admire the damned grain of their damned Eleventh Cycle damned inscription tablets!

* * *

Another thing about the charming and impractical Tarnisi, Krakar thought to himself with mixed feelings, was that they either all suffered from acrophobia or else believed it was impious for man to fly. He could think, at the moment, of no other reasons for having to spend an hour or more in a surface vehicle. The journey took them in a graceful hydrofoil craft, up an uneconomically curving river lined with trees of (he supposed) great beauty but no economic value whatsoever. "No, Master—tese trees no go-give resin-chop, no . . . Lumber-chop? No, not tat eiter. Only for go-look on, Master. . . ." Krakar was not much interested in trees that were only for being looked at.

Nor was he very much interested in the conversation of slow, whitebearded old Sapient Laforosan, who had devoted most of his life to cataloguing or lexicographizing the various Volanth languages or dialects. Evidently their host was not over-fascinated, either, for he said, "When you are utterly finished with that, Sapient, you'll turn your attention, I must hope, to doing similar work with the speech of dogs. I have, does it surprise the Sapient to hear? almost no desire to speak to or to be spoken to by Volanth. But I should love, I must hope, to understand what my dogs are saying."

Laforosan smiled and stroked his long white beard. "It is not always given to us to select our fields of interest," he explained. "When the lots were drawn at last selection, the black lot of Commercial Deputy fell upon you, my brother's child. My own involvement is of course not precisely the same. No fine to be paid to the State, should I refuse. But. . . . Well. . . ." He smiled again. "It began as I was painting leaves. My leaves, I must confess, were not much good, and, being young, I preferred to place the blame anywhere but on myself. 'I am bored with these local leaves,' I said. 'They are over-familiar and this is why they bore me.' So I went to the arboretum in Tarnis Town and to the arboretum in Thias Town and in Rophas Town and perhaps it may be that I no longer remember all of the places in which I painted the leaves of uncommon trees. It seemed to me that my paintings of leaves were getting somewhat better, and I must hope they were, for, after all, I was getting somewhat older!" He chuckled. The water hissed beneath the hull.

"But still I was not contented, and that is how I came to work my way out into the Outlands, I was seeking for new trees, you see. I found some. And I found something else, of course, as one is bound to in the Outlands: I found the

Volanth." Again he chuckled, this time perhaps with somewhat less mild good humor. "I heard them speaking to one another as they slashed the boles of the trees for resin. 'Speech?' I asked myself. 'Can this be *speech?* These animal gruntings and howlings? Surely they suffer some racial malformation of the organs of expression . . .' And there came to my mind that scene in the *Volanthani*—" He quoted words in the ancient tongue;

> " '*Thythat Léard Maddarydh
> Vholanth-querryl séith*—' "

Mothiosant murmured something, evidently the succeeding line; the old man nodded. "He saved the life of the Volanth pinned beneath the fallen tree, and the Volanth tried to warn him of the ambush. But Lord Maddary could not understand the language, and, as a result, he lost his only son. . . ." Laforosan gave a long sigh. "And thus it all began. I gave up trees and leaves and I took up tongues and languages. My painting chamber I converted into a study chamber, I got a license to allow three of them to come live at my place for a year—all stags, of course—and I got to work. It wasn't easy. Oh, they complained bitterly that their quarters were too clean, and it took about ten men to hold them down and clip their pelts . . . I wanted no little souvenirs, you understand. And their attention-span was about three minutes. But we began to make progress," and so the old man babbled on. And on.

Someone beneath the patterned awning on the aft-deck asked, after a while, "How many of these languages or dialects would you say there are, Sapient? You have found this out, I must hope, in all the years of study?"

"The answer really depends on classification. There are two main and one minor language groups, in a ratio—the approximate number of those speaking them—of about sixty, thirty-five, five. The two main ones seem distantly related, but the third is quite apart from them. As for dialects—" The boat seemed to give a slight lurch, there was a slight disturbance in the river, the old man frowned, paused a moment, someone above in the pilothouse laughed, the old man frowned, but continued to talk; and the boat went on. Scarcely a minute later, as they began to navigate yet another of the river's innumerable curves, Laforosan stopped, lifted his hand.

"Is anything not in total order, Sage?"

"That is so, and my plea is for you all to go inside and below immediately. Immediately, I must hope—"

But before any of them did so, the mud flats and shallows and river banks seemed to come alive. Things danced and shrieked and howled, a flock of small black birds rose and winged towards the boat.

Only they were not birds at all.

"Volanth! Volanth!"

Screams, scrambles, shouts, thuds, cries . . .

The boat trembled, careened, spun—

The boat continued round the curve in good order. Something had struck Krakar in the shoulder; the blow had sickened him a bit, but he could move hand and arm and had reason to believe nothing worse than soreness and stiffness would follow. But his outer shirt was mucky-black and rank smelling at that spot. All around him the fine Tarnisi had almost immediately recovered their poise. Even one, whose forehead trickled blood and mud, smiled at Ronk politely as their gazes met. In fact, all gazes seemed to meet his.

"We are ashamed, I must hope, that your first visit should be disturbed at all."

"Oh, my kith and kin! do, please, allow us to have your august shoulder examined!"

"Boy! Boy! Quickly go-bring clean clothes-chop for Bahon master!"

Bewildered, Krakar asked, "What *was* that?"

"Ground-apes. Man-pigs. Mother-maulers. In other words, Volanth," said one irascible and dirtied gentleman—who, a second later, recovered, apologized for his language. "Why? Ah, 'Why have they done so?' Who can say, my nephew's cousin. Last night there was a small shower of meteorites. They might, for all one knows, have thought that bad. And blamed it on us. And punished us for it."

But the old scholar, who had not moved from his chair, shook his head. "It was not that. And it may not be immodest, one must hope, to observe that the rogues know that they have at least one friend aboard: Has it been observed that this poor old student remains untouched? . . . The foreign guest asks, 'Why?' Here comes the answer—"

Pemathi deck hands pattered by, as swiftly as their burden would let them, burden with dragging hands and head laid open to the crushed bone, eyes staring futilely, blood dripping, dripping, drip. . . .

"The pilot boy. He broke up their fish weirs there, just above the bend. Needless. Needless. Even such creatures may eat, one must hope. Done for sport; surely it was not I alone who heard him laugh?"

Ah, the pilot boy. A crude Pemathi. The passengers clearly all felt better that the attack had been intended only for a Pemathi. "You don't mean, sir—or do you?" Krakar asked, bemused, "that at such a distance they can not only hit things, hit *people*? by thrown objects? but fatally? and can even avoid touching another individual person near by?"

Sapient Laforosan nodded. "Such is true. They have no other weapons. We allow them none. But with a stone or a shell or a stick, it is astonishing how, with their long arms, they can with precision strike and bring down flying birds and running game. It is perhaps their only art, poor rogues; well, one must not expect anything of them, they lack the Seven Signs, I must hope—well." He coughed in some embarrassment, source unknown to the Bahon guest; then, doubtless perceiving this, the Sapient went on, "They are really subhuman. There are morphological differences. The frenum under the tongue, for instance, which explains. . . . But digression must not persist: our ancestors, I should begin explanation, found them living in trees and caves, tried to teach them husbandry and crafts, soon found that there was a limit to their capacity of retaining knowledge, but none, alas! to their innate brutishness, decided henceforth to leave them alone to their cannibalism and incest. But again—and I say, again, alas!—this stern and meritorious isolation could not be maintained; it became necessary to set controls upon them. Difficulties, difficulties . . . still . . . this poor old scholar for one has not always found them utterly indifferent to favors shown. No. Only for the most part. We will talk of this at length, but another time, I must hope.

"Yellowtrees! Do you see?—up beyond the next bend? Have you never been there? You will enjoy your stay . . . one need not hope!"

* * *

Yellowtrees was more than the grove of flowering *ayilli*—unfortunately not then in bloom—which had given the estate its name. It was not an estate, as most were, which had come down in one family, generation after generation. Mothiosant's family's own hereditary lands had been escheated, forfeited, in fact, during political troubles a generation or two before; he himself had been born and raised abroad, wandering from place to place with his listless, disaffected father, homesick and yearning for the land unseen since childhood. Yellowtrees had belonged to another of the exiled families; its buildings and walks were famous. But that family had died out in exile. Mothiosant had returned . . . a very tentative return . . . to the homeland which he had never seen, when he was a young man. In point of fact, he had returned to nothing, but he found such welcome everywhere that he had volunteered to brave the outworld, the foreign lands, once more, to persuade others to return. He had been so successful in this, he had made such a niche for himself, had married so well and so nobly, that at length and not so very long ago, the Assembled Lords had granted him the tenure of Yellowtrees for his own lifetime. In a way, his occupancy of it brought him more éclat than if he had inherited it. There were apparant drawbacks . . . the Tarnisi had grown used to visiting it when it was a public place, and this habit still persisted . . . permission to visit could not tactfully be refused . . . there were often guests completely unknown to master and to mistress.

And it was one such guest who was the cause and center of an unpleasant incident on the second day of the Bahon's visit.

The lawn around the main house sloped down to the river in a shallow curve, but the back of the house overlooked not the river but a small stream which disembogued into it a short way below. At this point there was a walk of stone which led up two steps to the place where a bridge had been —but only the entrance pillars still remained; the bridge itself had been swept away in a long past freshet. Flowers, now, swept up to and around walk and pillars, frothing like many-colored waves. This scene was one of the well-known sights of the estate, as was the house itself, designed as it had been by that man of many parts, Sohalion, three centuries before. The reedy shallows where stream and river met, and the tiny wooded island nearby offshore, were always loud with the song and the cry of the birds which gathered there.

A light second lunch was set out by the soft-spoken, immaculate Pemathi servants, and the visitors—invited and permitted ones alike—were helped to it as a matter of course.

Mothiosant's young brother-in-law had been getting in some target practice with a spear-thrower before an audience consisting of his sister and her husband, the old scholar, the Bahon business agent, two old ladies, two young ladies, a middle-aged couple, a puffy-faced man who talked a trifle too loudly about the beauties of the estate—and, of course, the servants. Perhaps he had missed the precise center of the target once too often. The thrower, though it gave extra power to the spear, was long and heavy. Perhaps the audience had not been sufficiently admiring. At any rate, as the young man, his smooth strong chest shining with the sweat of his efforts, came up to the tables, his almost too-handsome face was rather sulky.

"Better luck another day, young cousin!" the puffy visitor said, his voice as always a bit over-loud, his remark calling attention to perhaps just that on which the brother-in-law desired least to hear comment.

He swung around so swiftly that the puffy-faced man jumped, gazed at the puffy-faced man with such naked scorn that even Krakar felt scorched by it, and said, almost spitting the words, "I'm—not—*your*—cousin!" Something seemed to crackle in the air. A Tarnisi insult? Was it possible? All present ignored what was occurring. All, that is, except the principals. The puffy-faced man seemed to sicken and turn pale. His tongue touched his trembling lip. The young man, after a long moment, turned away.

It might have passed over if the older man—he had a cup in one hand and a dish in the other—had found a seat and sat down and said nothing. But he did not. Almost uncomfortably openly attempting to change the subject, he said, inclining his head to the side, "How beautifully the sun shines through the branches of the trees." Or, at least, so it sounded to Krakar. But . . . again . . . something unspoken echoed in the languid air. And the young man turned back.

"What did you say?" he asked, as over-soft as the other had been over-loud.

The puffy-faced man now had himself under control. "How beautifully the sun shines th—" he hesitated—"in the foliage," he concluded.

"No . . ." said the brother-in-law. *"Not* what you said. '. . .The *bwanches of the twees* . . .' you said . . . Didn't you?" He took a step forward. The puffy man shook his head. He looked around him. The Tarnisi looked away. The Bahon looked on, uncomprehending. The brother-in-law took another step. Repeated, in a tone obviously peculiar but still completely baffling to the Bahon, " 'The *bwanches* of the *twees* . . .' " Then, in a suddenly changed, suddenly cheerful voice, "Do you not find it hot, my cousin? Eh?" The puffy-faced man smiled in sudden relief, but suddenly his smile trembled as the other raised his hands. "You *must* find it hot. And you all buttoned up and your august hands encumbered. Allow me," he said, voice begging, still moving forward, "to open your august shirt. Oh, do not step back. You will allow me the pleasure of assisting you, one must hope."

His hands darted forward, the puffy man jumped backward, stumbled, dropped cup and dish, stooped for them, jumped up, put his own hands to his shirt. A most curious look of shame, confusion, pain, and hate passed across his face. "Sick . . ." he muttered. "Sun . . . I must go. . . ." He bowed and bobbed hastily at the host and hostess, who still looked away, faces polite, absorbed, blank. "You will excuse me, I must hope. . . ." His voice died away. He turned and walked away, rapidly.

He had not gone very far across the lawn when the young man spoke, clearly, the single word, "*Quasi*." And the departing visitor's back started, arched, sagged, as though the young man had pierced it with one of his spears. A servant picked up cup and dish. The hostess made her first remark since the scene began.

"Destroy them," she said.

The old scholar rose, sighing deeply. "Allow me. Allow me. You will allow me to show the august visitors the nearer view of the river, I must hope." But host and hostess, rousing themselves, deplored the necessity of declining his offer. They must insist upon reserving that joy selfishly, they would escort the august visitors themselves. . . . In a moment only the old man, the brother-in-law, and Krakar remained by the refreshment tables.

"Is it to be believed?" the young man asked. "Is it to be endured? Is it not past time that something was done? They stone my brother's boat. They invade my sister's house. Oh—!" His face an almost tragic mask, his teeth chattered in an instant's uncontrolled rage.

"I do not under—"

"Volanth. *Volanth!*"

"But he was not—? He did not look—"

It was the Sapient Laforosan who undertook an explanation. "Ah, young foreign friend, it was in earlier days that our people cleansed their houses—it was cruel, true—by driving out the insane, the hopelessly diseased and immoral. They went into the wilderness and, shamelessly, they bred with the Volanth. The purge was hard, but it was necessary. We now have no more such amongst us. But you saw one of the results just now. A quasi-Volanth, carrying so many of the tainted Tarnisi genes that he thought himself able to pass as one of us. It was his tongue which quite betrayed him . . . though I suspected . . . as did this young man. Of course he did not wish his skin exposed to show him hairy as the other Volanth. A shameful incident. Too bad."

Krakar nodded. In this, as in all other things, the Tarnisi exceeded his understanding. Volanth . . . Quasi. . . . That look of shame and that look of hate. Those howling, naked figures in the river.

Those long and hairy arms, as strong as spear-throwers, which could hold no weapons other than a stone—and which, with stone alone, could be so vengeful. And so accurate.

CHAPTER THREE

Much of Lady Mani Itér oTor's past, as Jerred Northi had said, was either obscure or discreditable. Or both. But it was not doubted that she had validly married the sir Itér oTor, moribund scion of Pemath's moribund titled gentry, and this marriage had done wonders for her social status. The sir himself had since peacefully died and been buried with pomp and circumstance in his crumbling family mausoleum back among the Hills of Tor. Doubtless, the few remaining gentry, squatting and starving in their mouldering palaces, did not open their doors to the sir's widow. If this vexed her, which was unlikely, she did not show it. Her concern was not with any more of the past than could be of use to her in the present, and her present was in Pemath New Port. And there, amid the brash new villas and the ugly new blocks of flats, among the get-rich foreigners and the gotten-rich parvenus, Lady Mani, with her wealth and her title and her own innate cunning, made a mighty fine figure and did very well indeed.

So well, in fact, that she never appeared personally in either the front or even the rear offices of the "travel agency" at which Jerred Northi (hair dyed red, and almost buried in a back-country-cult burnoose) turned up two mornings later. The foreign clerk looked at him with controlled uncertainty. One never knew with these types—they might haggle forever over the cheapest passage to the nearest out-port . . . or they might bespeak the best accommodations available to the farthest Pemathi colony.

"What god-chop man go-want?" the clerk asked, civilly enough.

Northi showed him a card, took a number, sat down, fingered his hundred-bead rosary, from time to time glanced up and around from under his drooping hood. There were a number of well-nourished Pemathi, doubtless returning to jobs overseas from visits home, and now too high to resort to the native mass-passage companies. A polished-looking Lermencasi couple keyed their voices even lower than before as if to accentuate the difference between them and a Bahon engineer who was making a fuss about having to wait. An over-dressed tout, pretending to examine the posters, waiting to follow whoever left first. A few student tourers. The usual mixed lot. And then the clerk gestured to him.

One would not have thought that the agency would have had so many rooms in back of the front office. And certainly not that the "room" he was directed to was actually an elevator . . . not until the door closed behind him and the faintest of tremors advised him. It was, like the building itself (part of the complex Lady Mani holdings, no doubt), bran-new and up to date beyond comparison with Old Port counterparts. He did not know if he had gone up or down or how many floors. Then the door opened, revealing another room where a large, pale woman with close-cropped hair sat at one of those convenient desks which fold into the floor.

Walking in, he felt certain that this room too was an elevator. Convenient notion.

"There are lots of possibilities," the woman said, ignoring preliminaries, and allowing him to sit or stand as he might prefer. "Where do you want to go?"

"Tarnis."

"So would everyone else. Can't be done. Sojourners permits, we don't handle. Even if you could really pass for Pemathi. You really can't . . ." Something seemed to strike her mind.

She nodded. "Of course . . . that could be arranged . . . No. Makes no sense. What it would cost you couldn't be recouped if you served as a butler for a hundred years. If you could afford that . . . arrangement . . . why, fellow, the sensible thing is to go elsewhere with the money. Lermencas. Baho. Just about any of the islands. Besides . . . I said it could be arranged. I mean, it's theoretically possible. I'm sure it's not practicable, not actually possible. So.

"Now. Where do you want to go?"

"Tarnis."

She looked up now from contemplating her large, pale, clean hands, and seemed for the first time to consider him as a person. Not, of course, as a man. But as a person. "Fellow," she said, "you must be deep in bad trouble, or you wouldn't be here, trying to get out of Pemath. Pemath is where people come from everywhere else when they get deep in bad trouble *there*. And you must have a good portion of money, or you wouldn't have been sent to us, *here*. It goes without saying that you didn't inherit or earn it by dull, honest toil. So we may presuppose a certain amount of realism as part of your make-up." She sat back. He could hear the slight sound of cloth rubbing against cloth. It was a sensible gray cloth. She might have been a wardress in a very modern place of confinement in some well-run country.

"You know that Tarnis has the strictest immigration controls of any place on Orinel. Going there is, for you, out of the question. Except for Pemathi sojourners, who are allowed in as servants and skilled labor for a period of years, there *is*, in fact, *no* immigration to Tarnis. You know that, too.

"So. Now. For the last time. Where do you want to go?"

"Tarnis."

She nodded, unsurprised. "Let me see your hands and feet," she said. "All right," she said, after a moment. "It's not part of the regular service, you know. More's involved than forged papers and clandestine entrance, you know. A good much more . . . I hope you had something to eat before you came here because you won't get anything until they come to get you, and that won't be soon. I also hope you were careful not to be followed here, because if anyone comes looking for you: too bad. All right—you can go back in the other room and wait. If you know the words that go with those god-chop beads, you may not be bored."

He got up but didn't leave. Instead, he drew back the burnoose so that his face was exposed, but not his dyed hair. "Tell me if you remember my face," he asked.

She studied it a moment. "You were with a girl named Ko one night at that place I used to have down near Dock Ten."

"That's the only time?"

"Yes."

"Think hard. Try to visualize me as a child."

She stared at him with her blank eyes. "No . . . You're wrong. I've never seen you before. And whatever happens, I'll never see you again."

He turned and went out. The doors closed, the rooms moved.

It was quite a while that he was alone. Again and again he let the dull black beads slip through his fingers, but he didn't bother thinking about the words. He visualized her in her role as hostess to the flash, mixed world of Pemath New Port's gay society—painted hair and face, jewels and robes, music, crowds, noise, perfume, elaborate lunches and intricate dinners, games and races and all of that. . . . And then he pictured her, when the doors were closed at last, stripping off wig and gown and gems and washing away the false faces and looking down at the immaculate, plain, strong hands with which she did her filthy work: the sample which he had seen just now being by very far the cleanest.

She said she remembered him only as a man, and her memory was famous. She was not always, though she probably was now, the only child-hunt purveyor in Old Port. How old was she? He had no idea, but she had been around, though not as *Lady* Mani, as far back as he could remember. And how far was that? Twenty years ago, when the coffincraft *Italon* crashed in take-off—a convenient date—he had been fingering marks for Adán One-Eye, the pursepicker. Maybe he'd been a bit under ten at the time. No dates came to his mind before then, but there had been, there *must* have been a few years at least in Pemath before then. The trouble was, they were all jumbled together and he could never get them to come apart. There was an old woman who hit him often and then fed him well and another old woman who was often as hungry as he was but who was sweet and loving and wept much. The time the pot of boiling oil overturned and scarred his hip. A long procession through the narrow streets, lots of bright colors, sweets skewered on a stick, he and other dirty snottled brats dancing happily about. A boy with a harelip who shared a mouth piece of bread with him and died in his arms in a wind-scoured alley. Woods and trees, the green of them standing out in his mind as bright as scarlet for being the only ones he could remember until his teens, and could of course have been nowhere in Old Port. Probably the Parks of Don, the nearest ones, a half-day's excursion away, although the Parks never struck any chords of memory when he was there at later times; nor did he ever smell anything like the hot, herby scent always rising again whenever he thought of it. . . .

And as always, at last, the memory which lay underneath all other memories, the one he fought against, waking as well as sleeping—and fought against even now.

But even if Mani hadn't then gained control of all the kiddy fairs that early, if she'd been in that game at all she would certainly have attended the monthly auctions and must have seen him there. *If he'd been there.* It could be that she simply could not identify Jerred Northi, man, with the nameless and of course terrified child. It could be—could it be?—that she was lying. Why should she not?

Brooding on the bootless question of that, his defenses down, he was swept away once again, as always, by the hot, still air, and the hideously frightening and unfamiliar noises; he was running, running, running, they were behind him and beside him and then they were ahead of him and his head hurt his legs hurt his feet hurt, he dared not stumble, he turned aside, there was no background and no scenery, and he ran and he ran and he *ran*. . . .

"Steady on!" said the man who entered from the other "room," his arms full of packages. "I'm quite harmless."

Jerred stared at him. Of course he was quite harmless. It wasn't this monkey-faced fellow that made him jump to his feet with a cry of terror when the door opened. Or, not directly, it wasn't.

"—anybody who'd do that to a child," he said, thickly.

"I don't go for any of these mind-expanders," Monkey Face said, shaking his head, opening things; "they can expand you right out of your own, true skull. Shuck those ecclesiastical fantods, your reverence, if you please." He grinned.

Jerred wasn't convinced that the man was convinced it was a drug. It didn't matter, though. He disrobed, dressed in the clothes out of the boxes, after having submitted to a new complexion and a new face, new hair, and—once the tracheant was fitted in place where it wouldn't show—a new voice. It was all very effective, but—

"But will it get you where you intend to be going?" asked Monkey Face, reading his mind. Grinned again. Did it again. "No, I can't read your mind. But all the nods I take care of like this, they've all got the same own, true question. Answer is: No. It won't. Not intended to. But will get you to where you're going to do what *will* get you where you intend to be going. . . . Looks good on you. The perfect island-owner, up to spend the new crop money on a mad, flash whirl of the races, the river, the casinos, the hotels, and the flash, flash whorehouses—that's what you look like."

And may yet be, Jerred thought to himself. He took a last look at himself—sun-reddened skin, tan turban, tan tunic and shorts—and said, in his new hoarse voice. "I'm ready. Let's go."

* * *

"Yes, but why Tarnis?" asked the gentle voice beyond the very pleasant globe of kaleidoscopic lights. It was infinitely pleasant to lie at rest and watch the warmly-colored patterns change and change and change, slowly, slowly.

"Because it would be a waste just to run. Run I must, but if I must run, then let me run so as to get something besides just safety. Although it must stand to reason that Tarnis is safer than any other place worth being in. If it's hard for me to run there, it's hard for someone else to run after me there."

"And what's there that you want, besides safety?"

"Besides safety? Safety is there. I've been thieving and conniving all my life and all my ideas of success have been based on being a more successful thief. In Tarnis I wouldn't have to."

"How is that? Explain it."

Explain it? Was there anyone who didn't understand it? It was so clear and simple. Pemath was a dug that was sucked almost dry. If you wanted a drop of milk you had to fight your way to the udder, and, once there, you had to butt and bite. Tarnis was so full of milk it flowed out freely. You had only to lie down and lap. A rich land, underpopulated, barely exploited, indolently dealt with, yet strictly guarded. Tarnis was a land of legend and song and ease and treasures and all good things. "I've always been fascinated

34

by it . . . I think there's a fascination in it which is beyond my ability to analyze or to explain."

"Perhaps the fact is not at all like the dream."

This was not so pleasant. He frowned, lying in the luminous darkness. But not for long; after all, he had had the same thought more than once himself, and had answered it to his satisfaction. "Things to eat seldom taste as good as they smell, but they taste good enough, if they're good at all. The very servants return from Tarnis with their skins scarcely wrinkled and their hands scarcely soiled. Ten or twenty years there gives them enough in the Fiscal to live at their ease the rest of their lives. I could do better. I could do more, and I could do it in less time, because I would not be a servant, I would not be at the bottom, but at the top.

"I've been a rogue and a pirate because that was the way I found things here. All beyond the dreams of glory and wealth I have a dream of glory which lies in not being a rogue or a pirate, in not *having* to be one or the other. Doesn't the harlot dream of being a decent matron? Wouldn't the traitor prefer to be a patriot? In Pemath there isn't enough to go around. In places like Lermencas or Baho there *is* enough to go around—

"—But in Tarnis, there is more than enough to go around—"

The globe turned, the patterns changed, the colors swirled and melded. The bothersome image had been dissected, examined, expelled. It was cozy and content here, dreaming dreams of Tarnis. And the fulfillment would be better than the dream, for, after all, it was real . . . the dream was only a dream.

"Go on."

Success until now had always the taint and taste of slime about it. You climbed out of the muck only by planting your foot on the head of someone whom your climbing foot pushed deeper into the muck. You had to do it because there was no other way . . . except the way of being pushed into the muck by someone else's foot upon your head. It had to be so, here. It didn't have to be so everywhere. And the place it had to be so least of all: was Tarnis.

"I want to be rich more than I want to be decent. But that doesn't mean that I don't want to be decent at all. I do, I do! It's a luxury I'll be able to afford for the first time, in Tarnis. The Tarnisi don't want, particularly, to be rich at all. Of course they don't want *not* to be rich, they are rich without having had to do much to achieve it. They lie beneath the tree and catch the falling fruit. I wouldn't elbow them away. I wouldn't chop the tree down. I would gain more but they would not gain less. There would be less fruit left to rot upon the ground, but no one would be the worse for that. No one would suffer because I, instead of lying down, stood on my feet and plucked fruit still on the tree."

"You speak in metaphors."

He sighed, but it was a faint sigh. To explain was not unpleasant. "My metaphor means this: Given access to Tarnis and freedom in Tarnis, having been able to make money dishonestly in Pemath, I have no doubt of my being able to make money honestly and easily in Tarnis. They know nothing of commerce there. A little knowledge and a little effort should go a long, long way. Any vigorous outlander could do the same. I will do that and I will do it without doubts and contempts and recriminations and I will be happy while I do it. Allow me ten years or perhaps even five, and I'll have enough to retire for life."

"And where will you retire?"

Jerred hesitated.

"To one of the islands. There'd be enough for me to buy my own. Once I used to think of going off-Orinel, but not any more. I wouldn't want to range that far."

"But if Tarnis is or will prove to be so fine, why leave?"

There was silence, and the colored patterns shifted, shifted, like the swarming dances of butterflies. "I don't know," Jerred muttered after a while. "Somehow it always seemed to me that I'd have to leave. Maybe they wouldn't keep on liking me there, if they found out—I don't know."

The gentle voice said, *"These questions are not asked to annoy you, nor to make you engage in introspection which might conceivably be painful. In order for the Craftsmen to prepare you for your chosen goal they must know what, in general terms, you think about it."*

"And who are the Craftsmen?"

"Those who are to prepare you for your chosen goal. The demand is there, and it is we who meet it. It is our profession."

"And Lady Mani's—?"

"No. . . ." The voice was gentle as ever, not condemning her, not reproaching him. It might have belonged to one of those men the storytellers told about, men who were not men but man-like machines, "in the days of old, and in

former years;" ". . . *not Lady Mani's. She is merely aware of it, and receives her fee.*"

Well enough. This was Pemath. Nothing was ever done for nothing in Pemath. Although it was so pleasant lying here and doing nothing but watching the kaleidoscopic colors in the turning globe and dreaming wishful dreams. He rolled off the contoured couch and got to his feet. "I can't stay here forever, you know," he said.

"No. Of course not. We must begin."

Nothing in the voice altered. It gave nothing away. But Jerred Northi felt a sudden certainty that if he had not done exactly what he had just done and done it just exactly then, that he very well might have stayed there forever. Or, at least, that he would never have gone anywhere else.

* * *

"That's me for sure," he said.

Some of the mirrors were actually mirrors and some were 3D cameras and screen. Wherever he looked he saw himself, naked and alone. Life-sized, front and back and sidewise. Twice life-size, half life-size, all to scale, looking down views and angled views at level. A man in his late twenties, presumably, and in good health. Too dark of hair and skin to be Pemathi; too tall, as well. Tending to stoop, perhaps from an unwitting attempt to diminish his height to the average, perhaps influenced by the tendency of so many Pemathi to stoop even when not bowed by present and physical burdens; but not tending to stoop very much. Hazel eyes, mouth sullen more often than not, hairy in the usual places but not shaggy. In no way an outstanding body, but one familiar to him, one which had served him well enough.

And, "That's me for sure," a voice said, voice recognized after a moment as his own voice. Voice was well enough, too. Northi didn't know what others might make of it, but in it he recognized traces of all the nations and at least some of the other worlds who (for one) spoke InterGal and (for another) contributed to the population of the Two Ports; plus the subtle but unmistakable—at any rate, to him—influences of both Pemathi and the chopchop dialect which served as lingua franca. "That's me for sure"—loudly. "—me for sure"—softly.

Yes. Him for sure. And, unless he gave the word, him

never again more. Forever after his eyes would see someone else, his ears hear someone else, "Jerred Northi," in this physical identity, would have ceased to exist, and a stranger would take his place—a stranger to whom the man inside would have to become accustomed. Did he like the image of "Jerred Northi" enough to cling to it? He could, if he wanted to. He could then return to Lady Mani and be provided with papers and passage to Tannil or Mallasa or Ludens, Ran or Gor or Thonish, or any city or colony of Lermencas, Baho, or where he pleased. Anywhere at all. Only not Tarnis. Tarnis had never seen the body or heard the voice of "Jerred Northi" but was yet intent that it would never see or hear it. Tarnis he never knew. Did he want to know it enough to do this? To sentence "Jerred Northi" to death?

Vaguely, he wondered where the name had come from, who gave it to him and why? Someone with a sense of humor, evidently, for it was a Thonish name, and if one thing was certain from his physical appearance it was that he was not of Thonish stock. He had no sentimental attachment to the name, certainly, and as for the personality and appearance which went with it— He shrugged. He watched the shrug repeated in a variety of positions and sizes.

"I can do without Jerred Northi," he said. "Let's get on with it." The reflections, the images faded away. He made no particular effort to commit them to memory. There were a few pleasant memories. He supposed that he would remember them.

"Presumably," the Craftsman (He never learned any of their names, it being obvious that he was not intended to.) said, "the Tarnisi descend from a single small group of phenotypical progenitors. We know of no other people presenting so physically homogenous an appearance, or one— I'm speaking, naturally, of Orinel—whose appearance is so distinct from all other peoples. And inasmuch as everyone else seems always to have accepted them as a comely physical type, it's small wonder that they themselves are inclined to be exceedingly narcissistic. They speak about *the Seven Signs*. It's a dreadful, definitive reproach, no longer being confined to bodily appearance, for them to say of one of their number who has acted outrageously, *He lacks the Seven Signs*. In fact, even though the modern Tarnisi has studied anatomy and physiology and in theory knows better full well, his entire traditional training inclines him to regard the Seven Signs not merely as Tarnisi but as *human* characteristics. The inference is, of course, that the rest of us are really not quite human."

The Craftsman smiled. "As we see them seldom, and do not depend on them in any immediate way, we may find this amusing. It is understandable that isolation for so long a period, based upon the remoteness of their large island not only from other continents but even from other islands, should have increased (if indeed it did not produce) this tendency on their part. Isolation, plus the fact of their being so different in appearance from the aborigines of Tarnis . . . the Volanth. The Volanth were greatly inferior in culture and very different in appearance; furthermore, they were enemies. You see the logical equation. Different = Inferior = Dangerous."

His voice took on the smooth, confident, very slightly bored tone of the long-accustomed lecturer. "Fortunately, the introduction of Tarnis into the comity of nations occurred without violence or intrigue. Having no historical relation of enmity to the rest of us, they do not hate us. They do not even, as a general rule, despise us. But they cannot take us altogether seriously. After all, we don't know their language. We can't practice their arts. We engage in coarse activities like commerce—"

The man sitting in the hospital gown in front of him stirred, slightly.

"But, most important, most significant: *We lack the Seven Signs.*

"Do you see? Naturally, such creatures cannot be allowed unrestricted entrance into or access to one's country. And even the right to restricted residence has to be rigidly controlled. The only exceptions have been visitors on official missions, brief and ceremonial . . . visitors on commercial missions, suffered a short while in silence . . . and Pemathi. The Pemathi are there on sojourners' tickets—contracts, actually—for a term of years to perform certain specific tasks which the Tarnisi want done, but not enough to do them themselves. Most of the Pemathi, almost *all* the Pemathi there, are men. There are an allotted number of women, of course, because the Tarnisi realize that men need women and it would never do for the Pemathi to turn their attentions to Tarnisi women! But no sojourner ever stays to grow old there, none ever retire there, and if by chance or mischance one of their women should conceive, she goes elsewhere—any elsewhere—to have her child, and if she returns, she returns alone.

"Now—You have a question. Before stopping to answer it, I think I'd best enumerate the Seven—was that your question? I had an idea it was—the Seven Signs.

"Green eyes.

"Long fingers.

"Long ears, with tips.

"Smooth and hairless bodies.

"Full mouths.

"Slender feet.

"Melodious voices."

The atmosphere was like that of a small but very up-to-date and well-maintained medical centrum. Except that, at the moment, there seemed to be only one patient. "That's quite a bill to fill," he observed, quietly. He had seldom felt so passive, entirely submitting, in his life before. Perhaps never. He was no longer, at this moment, physically naked . . . but the tests and examinations he had been undergoing all day, and all day the day before, left him still feeling— he reached about for the thought—internally naked. As though everything about every cell of his body was now known and revealed, exposed.

The Craftsman at the desk said, "You have no idea, I think, just how large the bill is. But it may not involve endowing you with each and every one of the Seven Signs. As a matter of fact, not all of the Tarnisi by any means have all seven. It's the ideal of them which matters. As for you, we will see. . . . Which one of them, do you suppose, is the most difficult to achieve?"

The patient considered. "Oh . . . the green eyes, I suppose."

A brief smile rested on the Craftsman's thin, precise lips. "No. That will be the easiest. Fingers and feet pose the biggest problem, because there we are dealing with bone structure. Fortunately, you already have long fingers and slender feet. You were certainly aware that all of this has to be paid for," the Craftsman, changing the subject in so smooth and easy a voice that the transition seemed natural; "and that brings us to the matter of the price, which is 100,000 units."

"Yes, I . . . Oh. I haven't got that much. I never had."

"True. You have 35,000 in the National Fiscal, and three accounts under other names in other places which total 27,000 units. Your, ah, professional equipment we will not consider. Part of it belongs to your backers, and it will cause the least disturbance if we allow your crewmen to assume your equity for the present. There remains, then, personal property to the amount of 17,000 units; and all this comes to 69,000 units, or 31,000 less than is required. The Craftsmen will extend credit for the remainder. There is little doubt, we consider, that you will be paying it off before you leave Tarnis. We know what you have, what you have done, what you can do. It requires only a simple extension of logic to calculate, minimally, what you will do." He let out a satisfied breath. "And, if, after you leave Tarnis, you wish to assume another and different identity and form . . . the Craftsmen will make that possible for you, too." He looked very, very satisfied as he said this.

In the patient's mind, and, it seemed to him, in the very contours of the Craftsman's face and in the very molecules of the ambient air, the words took form: *And that will cost you more . . . much, much more.*

CHAPTER FOUR

Hob Sarlamat brought his hand up and out in the approved slow manner which avoided alike ungraceful abruptness and the possibility that his sleeve would ride up his arm and ruffle his cuff. "I have never seen the Tree of Consultation in finer bloom," he said.

"I suppose it's not more than three hundred years old," Atoral Tarolioth said, dryly. She made her mouth smaller, and glanced away when he looked at her.

"Really, Atoral, I am not *that* old," he protested.

"No, I believe that Tree is, let me see—it was planted by Tulan Soloniant in his third year as Guardian," the man on Atoral's other side said, considering. "Year ten, Cycle 80—"

Her full red mouth moved in silent amusement, then grew serious. "You know more than those of us who grew up being bored to the point of death," she said, "by tutors who crammed us full of facts."

He said, "My father often spoke of Tree and of everything connected with it."

"I can understand how the smallest detail can grow dear in exile.... Exile.... It will never happen to me, I must hope. Sometime, we must talk about—no. Forgive me. We will never talk about it. Let that die away from your memory, Tonorosant." She placed the tips of her fingers lightly on his wrist and looked up at him as though emphasizing that hers was no mere figure of speech, that she was in full fact asking a favor of him. There was something in this newly returned son of the exiles which was, well, *new*: and almost for that reason alone: interesting. A bit exciting. It was only by contrast with the occasional tartness of the exile's manner that the never-left-home people seemed, at least to her, Atoral, over-smooth and over-sweet. He returned her look. After a slow second they turned again to the great Tree, the convolutions of its great bole velveted with moss, its patterned leaves dipping up the sunlight, the great flowers of an intense crimson and an almost waxy texture. Sapient Laforosan had told them something of this species of tree before they had set out early in the morning to visit the most famous specimen. Even in its (within historical times) sole remaining habitat, high up in the hills and deep within the valleys of southern Tarnis—still largely Volanth country—the tree was rare. Looking at this one now, it seemed small wonder that even the brute Volanth held it in awe and conducted certain of their perhaps better left undetailed ceremonies beneath. This one in particular was planted by the famous hero Tulan Soloniant to commemorate his first victory over the Volanth, and the Synod of Guardians had met for many years under its then youthful shade.

At length Sarlamat smiled. "Enough. Or else we shall all begin painting leaves, and the air this morning is too crisp and delightful for such sedate pursuits. What shall we do now?"

"Swim," said Atoral.

They wandered down to the pavilion by the lovely little lake, paused to savor the scent of the frothy purple flowers in the reedbeds, tossed bits of food to the red-billed, black-winged lake birds. "Don't delay," she said, as they parted. Her words and smile were directed at both of them, but as Sarlamat turned away, once again she rested, lightly, so lightly, the tips of her long fingers on Tonorosant's wrist. Then she turned away, her brocaded skirt swirling.

The pavilion was dim and cool and smelling of wood and sap. Over the low partitions dividing the dressing-cubicles,

Sarlamat turned his rather prominent green eyes to his friend. "She is rather nice, I must hope," he said.

Tonorosant didn't answer the question.

"You're all right, I must—"

"Oh, yes, don't worry. My health, in mind and form, is excellent and will continue to be so, I must hope. I was preoccupied . . . By something for which I don't have a name. It's not confusion. 'Superimposition?' That's the closest. . . . I *do* remember my father telling me about Tree. I *do* that I don't remember any father and that if I did he'd never have heard of Tree. I *know* that it's perfectly proper to swim without clothes but that to be seen taking off clothes is embarrassing. And I *know*, also, that whether you are nude or clothed is merely a matter of having or not having money to buy clothes. I *am* aware that I spent the last two years as an underpaid free-lance teacher of Tarnisi in Ludens. And I am *also* aware that two years ago I never could speak a word of Tarnisi, that I have never been in Ludens, that I've spent that period of time cutting tows in the Inner Sea of Pemath.

"I can, very clearly, see the events in the life of Tonorosant. I know that I'm he. And yet, just as clearly, I can see and know that I'm Jerred Northi. And the two things are equally true and valid. Should I be afraid? Is there any chance that a time might come when one of these truths will fade away? Or vanish abruptly? And which one?"

Sarlamat shook his head. "No danger at all. No danger of either." He slid open the hatch, gestured Tonorosant to do the same. They went down the corridor, reed mats soft beneath their feet. "The hypno-indoctrination has never slipped yet. Should you even want to be entirely rid of either identity, why, that can be arranged. You were told it could. For the present, though, since you don't yet know just what you may want in the future, it's best to keep both. Do you think that *I* don't know just exactly how you feel? After all, I wasn't always Hob Sarlamat, anymore than you were always Tonorosant. But I've been Sarlamat for a good while, now. I was one of the first. Never had any trouble. Nor will you . . . and I needn't even add, 'I must hope.' Just remember, in case any blank spots appear, that no one will expect you to know everything. Your birth and bringing-up abroad will account for that. And also," he smiled, "I'm here, too. By and by you won't need me. Until then. . . ."

They came out into the sunlight and went down the

walk to the water. Atoral was waiting on the brim, her dark hair wound snug under the transparcap, her hands upon her golden hips. She smiled as they approached.

"Until then, it's best and easy, I must hope, for all to remain as it now does."

Tonorosant, who had been and in some way still was Jerred Northi, dashed forward, seized the girl in his arms and, he shouting, she screaming, fell sideways into the water.

She barely bothered to pretend offense. "This is not the way things are done abroad, I must hope," she said. "Did you treat the foreign girls this way?"

"Why should one bother treating them at all? They lack the Seven Signs."

They trod water. "And what do I lack?" she asked. She turned on her side and swam away. After a moment he caught up with her, and they made their way slowly and now sedately, side by side. With each stroke her breast lifted from the water for a flashing second, then was gone again.

"Why do you say that? I would say that you lack nothing —least of all, patience to endure my attentions."

This seemed to please her, he could see, but turning on her back and floating so, she asked, "Then why do you never see me alone? and always with Hob Sarlamat?"

He floated alongside her and he touched her. She moved closer. Surely, he thought to himself, a bit amused, a bit puzzled, but most of all, pleased; surely, she does not expect me to make love to her right here in the water, like the lake birds? He observed Sarlamat a good ways off and heading down towards the other end of the lake, doing a slow and classical stroke with many bobbings up and down. "He's not with me now—"

With pretended sulkiness, she said, "Why do you not go after him? I have heard of such things . . . abroad. . . ."

He touched her again, she gave a little scream, leaped around and struck him in the face with her flat hand, then darted away. For a moment he floundered, abashed, aghast. Then he swam after her. She was quick, though. She was very quick; he never did catch up with her in the water.

Afterwards, she said, as though to herself, and almost unwillingly, "So, then . . . not everything one learns in foreign parts is bad."

He thought that this required nothing to be said on his part, so he kissed her breast. It was still wet.

* * *

And even after that, though she no longer spoke of "having heard of such things . . . abroad," still she complained that he was often with his friend. He knew of no way to tell her that it was not quite so, but that his friend was often with him.

* * *

At various times in history the Synod of Guardians had been the supreme organ of delegated authority; at other periods this place had been occupied ("usurped," if one preferred) by the Assembled Lords. The sharpness of these historical dividing-eras was blurred by the often ages when the two had struggled for superiority without either quite gaining. The present governance of Tarnis was based upon a balanced and perpetual truce between them, a truce complicated in typical Tarnisi fashion by the fact of each body containing members who were also members of the other. The Tarnisi themselves accepted this, but not without a sense of its peculiarity—typified, perhaps, by the famous story of the young man who—facing a parental summons to account for reported wrongdoing—urgently inquired of his mother, "Advise me, for my life! is my august father being a Lord or a Guardian today? so that I may know what to say to him!"

That young Lord Tilionoth was among the informal gathering at Greenglades, when everyone was concerned with matters affecting the interest of the Guardians, was no surprise either to him or to the others. It was the season of the Former Equinox and green was being worn: leaf-green, grass-green, sea-green, sky-green, grain-green, insect-green; sunset-, dark-, and feather-green. Tilionoth had removed his robe of vine-green and stood in under-costume of the same hue, a hundred marks from the great triangular target, the figure which had once delineated a stag-Volanth prancing with club in hand now faded to a dim outline on which only the five vital spots—throat, heart, belly, and the arteries of the right and left groins—still stood out brightly and retouched. The young Lord moved up and down on his toes and swung his arms. His Pemathi handed him the spearthrower and he held it with his right arm and placed it athwart his right shoulder. Next he took the target spear, examined it, hefted and tossed it several times, catching it with his left hand. Then he stepped back to the line and set

45

the shaft in the thrower so that the butt end rested securely in the pocket prepared for it at the end of the throwing-stick.

Several of the older men leaned upon their T-staves and watched with detached interest.

"Stands well. . . ."

"Yes. None of those ropy muscles, you know. Ah—"

"Well tossed! Well thrown! Neatly in the left!"

"Glad to see that his fondness for foreign toys hasn't made Tilionoth forgetful of the classical sports."

"Ah—! Neatly in the throat! Well tossed!"

"What foreign toys are those, Guardian?"

"Oh. . . ." The gray-haired Guardian waved his hand downslope. "You know. The river, there, for instance. Skimming and darting like water-bugs, hundreds of them. You can't have missed them."

"Yes, yes. Those tiny power craft, the one-man ones? I've been tempted to try, but I've got too much belly on me to lie flat, and then, you know, all that spray in the face, I. . . . Neatly in the right!"

"Well tossed!"

The few women present waved their hands so that their jewelled bangles tinkled like tiny bells. The air smelled of fresh-cut grass and of the aromatic sawdust sprinkled at the line where Lord Tilionoth stood, now swinging the thrower in his right hand to limber it and the arm and shoulder muscles. He glanced at one of the women and smiled.

"There's been quite a fashion for foreign toys of late, it seems to me. It won't result in any turning away from any of the ancient ways, not just in sport, one must hope. Ah—! Ah—! Neatly and well!"

The gray-haired Guardian placed two fingers before his lips in the Tarnisi negative. "Oh, no fear of that, no fear. One of the returned men, son of an exile, Tonorosant—have you met him? You will, one must hope—he has sort of taken up these foreign toys as a hobby. And, well, one does know that none of us born in the land are ever so anxious for the ancient ways as a returned exile. Which is understandable, which is natural . . . deprived of them for so long, '*in barbarous lands and far*,' oh?"

" '*Thirsty flock, return ye to the water*,' oh?"

"Just exactly. . . . Ah. Last shaft." They placed the carved and gilded top-pieces of their T-staves securely under their arms and leaned forward, mouths slightly open, jaws thrust slightly forward. No arm unaided could ever have propelled a target-spear one hundred marks; this was the function of the long wooden spear thrower, to constitute as it were an artificial extension of the thrower's arm, thus to give greater force and distance to the hurtled lance shaft. A very light sweat glistened on the sun-dark skin of Lord Tilionoth, on face and neck, hands and arms and lower legs. He stood for a moment motionless in his place, the thrower hanging from his one hand, the spear pointing head down as it rested loosely in the other. In one swift flashing series of motions which seemed almost one motion, spear was in spear-thrower and thrower was flung forward and downward and spear was in air and spear was transfixed in target and quivered there and Lord Tilionoth was just righting himself and the *thud* of the stricken board met their ears.

"Heart! Heart! Well tossed, well thrown, and neatly in the heart!"

The dim and dancing Volanth image supported five shafts. Not one had missed, not one had dropped out. "No fear, eh? that anyone who can throw like that is likely to be spoiled by foreign toys—"

"None whatsoever, one must hope. Mmm. Umm. Tilionoth is, ah, still quite safe?"

A look of craft and cunning and pride passed between the gray-haired man in the dark-green and the ruddy-faced one in the lizard-green robe, swept down to cover the young spearman who, stripping off his dampened under-tunic, was walking towards the bathing-booth, and came back to each other.

"Oh, yes. Still quite safe, one need not hope."

Something of the heat had begun to pass from the later afternoon air. The groups of spectators broke up, walked to and fro, formed into other groups, gradually dispersed. And still the two stood where they had stood, leaning each one upon his T-stave, talking in tones no less intent for being quiet. And at length even they turned and tucked their staves and slowly walked back to the great bulk of Greenglades, greener—beneath its clustering of thick-growing vines —than the robes of either. They had mounted the low rise just before the ramp when one of them stopped and took a bit of the other's sleeve between his thumb and his forefinger.

"One moment more, my sister's sib. . . ."

"Certainly . . . ? my brother's get. . . ."

"In all our talk of those men long-known and familiar to

us, let us not forget the newly re-arrived. Exiles need not necessarily assume their fathers' and grandfathers' allegiances. Do you follow? So. And there is this, too, that their former lives abroad have served to whet their wits and sharpen their—"

The other nodded, once, twice, quickly.

"Yes. There *is* that. Toys or not. Let us indeed not forget it."

They walked their separate ways into the house.

* * *

Tonorosant and Sarlamat stood looking over the railing of Tonorosant's new house at the swift-flowing river where the water purled among the grasses of the shallows. Not far below, it curved and vanished among clumps of furry saplings and beneath overhanging branches of huge-boled trees. A water-wander flipped and dipped after sprats in the eddy, sending scattered drops to pierce the pattern of the ripples. Now and then came a sound of wooden bowls clattering from the kitchen, almost instantly hushed by the soft-voiced and soft-footed Pemathi house servants. Aside from this, the sound of the water, and an occasional flash of bird song, all was silence.

Tonorosant sighed and breathed deeply. "I hope that no one is ever bored with this," he said. "The river. . . . A whole new, clean, vivid, sweet, wonderful world. The river at Old Port was an open sewer, it didn't even have tide enough to keep it clean. I saw the body of an infant floating there once, I remember. Came back a week later, it was still there." He grimaced, shook his head and shoulders. Then he turned to his friend.

"How is your new lady?"

Hob Sarlamat smiled, the lines about his full mouth deepening. "She is well, she is wonderful. We are good friends, very good ones. She now accepts the fact that I don't and never will paint leaves well, and of course blames it on my foreign upbringing. And I of course don't bother to explain that I simply have no interest in painting leaves. Some things sink in more than others, I suppose. But I am in no hurry to leave, you can understand."

"I do, I must hope," said Tonorosant, who had been Jerred Northi. And, in a way, still was. "Atoral is coming for supper and she will stay the night."

Sarlamat murmured, How nice. He smiled again. He made no move to leave.

"—And. I don't know if you were informed . . ." Tonorosant knew, in fact, almost nothing of the subtle means whereby Hob was kept informed. ". . . but I have paid the last amount. To the Craftsmen, I mean. I now own myself." It was his turn to smile. He saw his face reflected in a little pool below. It was a well-made face, in more senses than one, and he liked it not the least because it lacked a certain pinched, bitter look which the face of Jerred Northi had been sometimes wont to have. He admired in a detached way the line of the upper eyelids, in between acanthic and epicanthic, and the way the green of the iris took on a deeper green from the water.

"Congratulations," Sarlamat said, in his low, slow, unhurried voice. "On 'owning yourself,' I mean. It was a good stroke of business, wouldn't you agree? Yes . . . you no longer need me. You haven't for quite some time now. As far as that's concerned I could leave. But . . . I rather like it here, do you know," he smiled. "And in addition to everything else, there's my new lady. So I am in no hurry."

His friend disclaimed any desire that he should ever be in any hurry to leave. Somehow the talk fell upon the subject of "foreign toys," as the Tarnisi had from the first chosen to call them. There were the water sleds which had set at least half of the younger male Tarnisi skimming and darting over rivers and lakes. The great, kite-shaped gliders which had made so great and so unexpected an appeal to the older members of the community, with their slow, silent, majestic soarings and swoopings, rich—it turned out—in philosophical over- and undertones. The coiffures, available in at least a hundred different models, undistinguishable by touch and sight from natural hair, which released the mature and elder matrons from the hours of tedious setting and waiting previously required to procure the results demanded by inflexible and unchanging tradition which had almost the force of law. And all the others. . . .

And still it passed off without difficulty as a mere hobby of Tonorosant's, he helping to gratify the curiosity of his fellow-elite with foreign-acquired acumen. The stigma of commerce was not present. The open work of importation was arranged by his Pemathi clerk and distribution carried on between the latter and the clerks and stewards or other upper servants of the Tarnisi interested. Openly, the once

Jerred Northi never touched money. No one insulted him by asking a price, he insulted no one by naming it. In all probability, no one but the Pemathi under-class was even aware that he was making money. The mind of aristocratic Tarnis was simply not attuned to thinking along such lines. The Pemathi, of course, knew. They had the task of paying out their master's money, after all. Which made them, likely, the most pleased of all; for it was a firm principle of their homeland's that "money must melt." And it melted a little in every pair of pale, red-haired, often freckled hands . . . to freeze up again until it should be time to retire to Pemath and melt (or at least thaw) all over again.

Meanwhile, in several various foreign fiscals, Tonorosant's personal (and exceedingly private!) accounts went on to grow and proliferate in a most satisfactory manner.

Atoral came and dined and stayed the night and her lover wondered again about the Tarnisi prejudice against early marriage . . . "early" being anything before the middle thirties. In general it had, he supposed, the virtue of keeping down the numbers of the Tarnisi population, although certainly sophisticated methods of doing so were not only known but utilized . . . as, for example, by Atoral. Prejudice, again, tended to disallow its use within the marital structure. And in particular it enabled him, Tonorosant, to enjoy the pleasures and benefits of the liaison without worrying about the entanglements of marriage. Which could become very entangled indeed. His genes had not been changed by the processes he had undergone at the hands of the Craftsmen. Such change was possible, or had at least once been possible. But Orinel was not a world in which the fullness of the possible had ever been used to flourish. Tarnisi reaction to his fathering obviously only half-Tarnisi children would be unfavorable, to say the least. It would not only be infinitely unwise for himself, it would be infinitely unfair to both the woman and the child. He recollected with distaste the incident he had been told about of the "Quasi" who had tried to pass as pure Tarnisi that day at Yellowtrees . . . and all the incredibly ugly talk about such wretched creatures which from time to time cropped up in conversation. And then there was the merely emotional matter of his becoming over-involved with Tarnisi life at all.

No, no. Better to remain disengaged as most he might, and then, when he judged it best, slip out and slip away and simply never return, leaving behind him nothing deeper than perhaps casual wonder.

Meanwhile, if Atoral had accepted wonderingly certain aspects of physical lovemaking which Tonorosant had not learned in Tarnis, it was his part to accept with perhaps less wonder but no less appreciation certain aspects which she had certainly learned nowhere else. The chamber still odorous of the fresh-worked and fragrant wood, her body unworn and pliant in his arms, her voice joyously astonished in his ears, her hands sincere and deft upon his skin, were all quite and excellently different from either the stews of Pemath Old Port or the fancier brothels of the New Port or the either bluntly commercial or rough liaisons he had had elsewhere. There was no striving without desire on either his part or hers, no mere sufferance by her, no mere seeking outlet and relief by him. Repetition did not satiate either before the other and both were spared the near-Hell into which near-Heaven may so easily turn or be turned when appetite and its quest is all one-sided.

The deadly words, *You think only of your own pleasure,* had never passed in voice or thought between them.

They arose and walked about the grounds in the coolness of the dawn and the dew. His tentative identification of certain plants amused her, his absolute ignorance of some several others dismayed her. "Exile must be quite dreadful," she said, her humor passing into genuine feeling.

"It is. . . ."

"To have no home, no family, no scenes so necessary that they cannot be done without—I can't know how that might be."

"No," he said, a bitter, sombre note penetrating his thought and voice. "You can't. Be glad."

She bent to touch a flower and watch the drops of mist distill down its petals. Her face in profile seemed incredibly delicate and young. And lovely, too. He bent and touched her lip, her cheek.

"Oh, stay today. You will, I must hope?"

She smiled gently, but was so firm that regret could not enter. "Not be present at the *tulsa*-festival of my aunt's youngest daughter? You aren't serious, I must hope. One reaches puberty only once, you know. I remember my own. . . . I would ask you, you know, but we haven't been lovers quite long enough. But I'll return tonight. Will I be welcome?"

He spent the morning going over accounts with Idór uDan, his ostensible personal steward but actual executive vice-president. Long familiarity with the Pemathi mind and method made it unnecessary for him to reveal that he knew both chopchop and the actual language; the figures in the records and a very few words sufficed them both—and sometimes only a look, a clearing of the throat, a tap of the finger was sufficient. It was far from likely that Idór uDan believed that his employer's interests in "foreign toys" constituted no more than a hobby. There was no cause for concern. 'Dan was in Tarnis for the exact same purpose as his master: the "pure and disinterested desire" of making money: and would keep silence all the days of his life for the sake of ten tickys . . . let alone the hundreds of units which the matter would bring him. A passenger by grace and favor alone, he was not one to risk rocking the boat.

It was after a lunch eaten leisurely on the front slope of his house, dressed with brief, flitting, recurrent memories of dirty three-dish dining rooms, that he had changed his clothes with the intention of taking the prescribed two turns around his grounds. The upper houseboy appeared and, bowing silently, held out to him a T-stave with something bright wound about the crutch of it. The silver shoulder loop and crest of formal-most attire. This was high courtesy indeed: for every-day formality was abundantly satisfied with a rectangular card on which the crest was enprinted. He looked at the servant. "Guardian Othofarinal," the man whispered. Tonorosant reflected a moment. Then he removed it. This was in effect an invitation for the owner to enter, for, according to ceremonial theory, he could not proceed away without it. One was in effect compelling him to enter. The servant bowed again and made to withdraw.

"Wait." Tonorosant went into his cabinet room and removed from the wall chest the small inlaid box containing his own silver shoulder loop and crest. Returning, he wound this around the crutch of the T-stave, gestured the servant to present it to the caller. This was a double invitation to enter, implying as it did that the master of the house deprived himself of the possibility of leaving it unless he who received it returned it . . . by his own hand, of course. Then he withdrew to change into formal dress: robe, ruff, hood, gloves; and when the servant returned with the Guardian, he, Tonorosant, the master of the house, bowed, and accepted as though it were a great gift the fastening of his own silver crest loop upon his shoulder.

Guardian Othofarinal was gray of hair and grave of manner. The gravity, however, was in no way a cold one. "I had heard," he said, as they sat together over the half-emptied ritual glasses of greeting, "that you were scrupulous in observing the classical ways, and I am more than pleased to see that you are in this respect more than scrupulous. Evidently your late and august father must have been exceedingly careful to instruct you during your unhappy years amongst those who lack the Seven Signs. Thank you for receiving my offer of visitation as you did. It encourages me to proceed more directly to my subject than I perhaps otherwise would."

"You will certainly do so, I must hope."

He did. The subject of the Guardian was that of Tarnisi policy towards the exiles. Until now the policy was that there was no policy. Exiles were free to return, many had done so, moved by their individual urges or by the solicitation of other individuals. But it was altogether an individual thing. This, the Guardian suggested, ought not to be. The official and collective policy of the Governance of Tarnis should be, firstly, to invite all exiles back to the home of civilization; secondly, to assist their passages and to relieve their immediate needs; and, thirdly, to provide them with the means to occupy without embarrassment or difficulty their appropriate places in society. "You may agree with me, I must hope?" the Guardian concluded.

"I should and I do, my father's brother."

Othofarinal inclined his head, brought it up again so that he was face to face with his host. "Then may I venture to suggest to a small number of my friends who are of a like mind that we may arrange for all of us to meet and to discuss this subject? Your experiences will add an essential reality to a matter which none of the rest of us know by our own experience. You will consent, I must hope?"

He consented to walk about the grounds, he approved of what he saw, and he gave good advice about the erection of out-buildings and the planting of trees, "—so that the leaves will show to best advantage at sunrise, sunhigh, and sunset, according to classical methodology. . . ."

Atoral returned at night as she had said, and was followed in moments by Sarlamat—whom she was not overjoyed to see. The poise appropriate and customary to a Tarnisi seemed now stretched rather thin in her manner as she asked pointed questions about Hob's lady and why she had been left alone, commented—stiffly—that Tonorosant did not abandon her, Atoral, to go and interpose himself between the other lady and her lover. As much to change the subject (Hob, however, not rising to be baited, merely smiling, casually, smiling) as anything else, Tonorosant told at some length of his afternoon's visit and visitor. Atoral's reaction surprised more than it gratified him.

She struck her hands together twice, cried, in obvious dismay, "Oh, *why*—why! did you say that? To agree to his plans? Don't you see how he is using you?"

"No, not at all. I don't see . . . how . . . ?"

"They do not care a snap for the exiles' welfare. It's all just a political gambit. When most of you—your fathers, then—were gone abroad, the Assembled Lords were the powerful party. Naturally it was they who had the dividing and allocating of the abandoned lands, the houses and estates. Naturally they helped their friends liberally. It is the Guardians' intention to deprive the Lords in the name of helping the exiles! Can't you see what turmoil this will create?"

He did, most clearly. "The last thing I want is to become involved in factionalism, I must hope," he said, frowning. "I will send to tell him so."

She smiled her relief, he smiled to see her smile. Then Sarlamat got up, crossed over, said firmly, "No, my mother's child, you must and will do nothing of the sort."

"Why not?"

"Why not?"

Sarlamat's smile was briefer now, and no longer casual. "Because," he said, "it would hurt the exiles most of all. Few of us were able to be leading lives of honorable leisure in foreign parts. Most of us were obliged to lead lives and to do things which could not easily be either understood here nor excused. I am certain, Tonorosant, that your withdrawing from the Guardians' efforts would create a breach which would have to draw attention to the exiles in greater detail than would be at all comfortable. This will not happen, I must hope." Atoral made impatient noise and gesture, but Sarlamat was ignoring her—and yet not ignoring her at all—as he went on to say, "There are interested parties and there are other interested parties. Some of them are less reluctant to reveal embarrassments than others. No. No, my mother's and my father's child. You will not escape one faction by fleeing into the arms of another. I can assure you of my certain knowledge of the fact that those to whom you have most reason to be grateful would not want you to.

"No, they would not. I swear it. I swear it by the Seven Signs we bear on our bodies . . ."

Their green eyes met in a long and loveless look.

CHAPTER FIVE

Tarnis Town clustered and glowed like a nest of jewels, domes and arches and music towers, ruffed about with gardens and with flowering trees. Tonorosant glided along on his tiny, scarlet, steam float and turned into the pond-spangled grounds of the Commercial Delegation. The Delegate himself, Mothiosant, received him alone in his office. His manner was strangely simple, strangely cold with an inner rather than outer chill, utterly simple.

"There are three men coming from over the sea," he said, "and you are to host them for the time being."

No polite murmurings of kinship terms, no civil expressions of I-must-hope.

So, though much astonished, Tonorosant said, equally simply, "I have other things in mind, and I don't understand if I'm being asked or commanded. And if commanded, then by whom? Surely not you?"

Mothiosant said, "You were helped. Now you must help." He looked at him, looked through him, looked away from him.

The chill was infectious. Feeling a slight shiver, a slight shudder, sensing rather than believing the unnamed inference, Tonorosant protested, "My debts to those in Pemath have by now been fully paid."

Mothiosant lifted his dark and massive face. He smiled, thinly, briefly. "Such debts are *never* paid," he said. "I paid mine a long time ago. But it is still not paid, do you see."

There was no threat here. No warning. Just a simple statement of fact. "So . . . you, then, are the same as I. . . ."

The Commercial Deputy flicked his hand, as though to

say: Of course. What then? What of it? Don't be obvious, it is boring.

"You are. Well. What . . . do the Craftsmen never let go their grip?" asked the younger man.

"No, never. Why should they? Each link draws the next, and so the chain moves on. There is even a moral justification to it, if I must hammer the point home once again. *You were helped. Now you must help.* Of course, for them, it's just a matter of business. So—we now return to the beginning: There are three men coming from over the sea, and you are to host them for the time being."

Jerred Northi, annoyed, angered, dismayed, sank beneath the surface. Tonorosant, poised, suave, submissive, rose from out it. "Indeed, my father's sib, they will look upon my house as their unique own, I must hope." He bowed.

* * *

When it came to it, though, the three men dwindled into one man, one young man. Tonoro had said something about wishing that he had been supplied, in that case, with a young *woman*. . . . Mothiosant merely grunted, Sarlamat smiled, shook his head. The services of the Craftsmen did not, evidently, extend to the female sex—at least not as far as Tarnis was concerned.

The young man's name (name from now on, at any rate) was Hob Tellecest. Tonoro wondered if he himself could ever have been so young, so delighted, so stricken with awe and novelty. Probably not. He had not only been older in years when the Craftsmen processed him, he had been much older than his years as far as experience and attitude was concerned.

He met Hob Tellecest on the threshold, bade him formal welcome. "Tarnis!" said Hob Tellecest.

He showed him his rooms, begged him to say immediately if there should ever be anything he desired which was not at once to hand. "Tarnis!" said Hob Tellecest.

Tonoro took him about the grounds, showed him the river, spoke to him of this and that: all that Hob Tellecest said, or, evidently, was able to say, was, "Tarnis!"

By and by, though, although he still seemed in many ways like a newborn creature bemused by the richness of the world of light, he found his tongue. "It's not a dream . . . no, it's really true. I'm really in Tarnis . . . ."

"I, too, am rather fond of it. The pleasures of the return do not, indeed, make the exile worthwhile. But they sweeten the bitterness of the memory."

The look his new guest gave him had nothing of irony in it. Nothing but agreement. Understanding. Accord. He was so young, so touchingly enchanted, so grateful, that Tonoro's resentment quite died away. But, like a child's fulcrum board, as one side dropped, the other side rose. Was it really for money alone that the Craftsmen held on so, never letting go? It could hardly be. They did not, could not depend on word of mouth advertising by satisfied, Tarnis-endenizened, clients. And if there was a part of their system which was not based on money, might it not be that other parts of it were not based on money either? And, if this were so, then the possibility was a decided one that *no* part of it was based on money.

In which case the money paid to them was not a fee at all—but a pretext. The supposition was an interesting one, but when he asked himself, "Pretext for what?" he discovered no answers. So there was nothing to do but to shrug, and to do his best to make the young man more and more familiar with his new country. He never asked him what his old country had been, or why he had left it. Such questions, it was clear, never were asked. The reason for this was of the best, of course; he hardly desired that anyone be tempted to ask the same questions of him!

It did not escape his attention that in making acquaintances for Tellecest, he made them, also, for Tonorosant. Friends introduced friends, kinsmen desired to—and did— make him known to other kinsmen. *Each link draws the next, and so the chain moves on.* Mothiosant's remark was proving to be perfectly true. But why the chain was intended to move, or why it existed at all: this he had yet to learn.

The thing he was next to learn had nothing to do with any of this. The Volanth—the word flashed like heat lightning, echoed like thunder—the Volanth had risen in revolt. And, as neither he nor Tellecest had ever served on a military levy, both were called out on duty to suppress it.

* * *

The country they were passing through, the lower Outlands, was sun-scorched and sullen, low and rolling hills and much flat terrain, broken often by dry river beds. Trees were few. The crops had already been gathered and nothing was seen in the fields but ragged stubble and here and there the swift, secretive movement and sudden, covert stop of some lizard-like creature or such small vermin. It was not a friendly terrain, not a happy one. Something harsh and nasty seemed to emanate from the hot, cracked earth . . . something droning and hateful.

"What do you think, Tonorosant, of all this?"

He looked briefly at the questioner—a lacklander named Cominthal—and shrugged. "I will do my duty, I must hope," he said.

The floats hissed lightly, stirring up a faint dust as they sped along. Cominthal made a wry mouth. "You talk like a book of maxims. Page one, line one. That's not what I mean. I—well. You will see soon enough."

He saw sooner than any of them thought. The levy-lord in charge of the hundred grunted, gestured with a sweep of his hand; instantly the formation spread out into the form of a wide, thin crescent as they turned on a left oblique angle. The river beds, no longer full dry, converged into a sort of fen, full of tangled brush and towering plants and here and there a smear of flat green. Cominthal pointed out one of these. "Looks like good grassy turf, doesn't it? Be nice and springy underfoot, you think?"

Understanding, obviously, that it was—must be—nothing of the sort, but wishing to allow the man to make the point himself, Tonorosant civilly said, "One would think so."

"Oh, would one?" the lacklander sneered. "Then try it. Oh? Try it? No? Feet not so brave as mouth?"—then, as though losing interest in baiting him, or perhaps not wanting to try it too far, abruptly said, "Just don't try it, brother-in-law. It would suck you in like a bubble of snot." Once again and instantly his manner (if not his mood) changed, and he said, with a slight bow, "You will excuse the coarseness of my metaphor, I must hope. Sallying among the Volanth does little to promote the subtler niceties." It was well done, of its kind. Draw your man out, let his decency involve him, cut him off, rub his face—then withdraw so that your tracks were covered and he could not follow.

Tonorosant should have liked to have tripped him off the float over the next green patch and seen him sink into slime over his sneering face. Of course it was not worth the try or thought. So, still civil, but with a hint, perhaps, of bugger-me-not in his voice, he said, "Thanks for your warning. My eyes will be always open . . . and my ears, too. . . ."

The lacklander carefully read nothing from or into this, but cleared his throat and looked away.

They passed fetid marshways where the earth seemed flatulent, and choked ponds iridescent with scum. "Don't say that people can live in these places?" Tonorosant asked after a while.

The levy-lord heard him, scowled. "People, not people, no," he replied without looking over. "Just Volanth. This is what made them . . . beds of warm muck, fermenting forever in the sun until the first ones crawled out up on the land to dry— Over. Down." His voice fell to a whisper, his hand to an outstretched, downward-pointing claw. The formation wheeled, circled, closed.

"First fruit of the harvest," someone said in a thick mutter.

She lay on her back, looking at them, one hand entangled in her dress, as though trying to pull it down. The initial glance fled at once, was forced back: *She's black, she's not from here,* was his startled thought. Realizing at once that the sun had made her so, realizing at once that she had not really winked at them. There was a maggot in her eye. There were maggots crawling in both her eyes, and in her ears and mouth and nostrils and in her vagina. The blackened skin had cracked as the corrupt flesh had swelled, revealing the yellow layer of fat beneath. There was a taste of bile in his mouth and the muscles of his chin tightened for a moment against overwhelming nausea. Then the moment passed.

He looked quickly at the other, circling faces. Here a mouth lay open, there one sagged loose and dull, some were blank as dumb masks, others almost bright with fierceness. "That dress," the levy-lord said. He hawked something from his throat, turned aside and spet out behind covering hand. "You won't see cloth like that on just any bitch-Volanth. She was a licensed servant, I suppose, to one of ours . . . and that's why they served her as they did."

Cominthal yawned, choked it abruptly. "Let them serve her as they like, and who gives a crack? Let's get on and find out what happened to the people she worked for—" Rather too quickly, rather too fawningly, he added, "The august levy-lord agrees with me, I must hope."

The flies had settled back, buzzing, only to rise from the ravaged corpse again as the floats sped off without a backward look. And now the hundred was a long drawn-out line, each man scanning the ground with fierce concentration. It did not take them so very long to find the probable scene the Volanth woman had been fleeing away from when caught. But they might have dawdled by her longer, taken, even, had the ancient ways so much as considered—let alone demanded it—time enough to tip that first body into a hasty-dug grave, for all that speed had done of good.

There was a woman here, too, and her garments had been made of richer stuff yet . . . by the fragments of them that lay about . . . by the blood-stiff fragments of them. And onward a ways was another woman, an older one, but her age availed her nothing. And last of all, fallen with his back towards the woman whose flight he had futilely defended, was the man: presumably husband and son, or son-in-law. Evidently they had started to flay him alive with sharp shells, but interest had flagged—perhaps when he was dead, perhaps only some time afterward. Behind them, as the men of the levy passed backward and forward, first cursing, then grim, they saw the trail of things so hastily snatched up . . . and doubtless even more hastily dropped as pursuit grew fierce and hot. A garment. A blanket. A bag of food. Things never put to use, except, of course, to help track them down.

Then there was a cry like a groan. Someone pointed. Someone winced. Someone turned away. Someone hissed in bared teeth.

A toy.

It was harder finding the child, he had been hidden well, and evidently, whether obedient to a half-understood command, or understanding nothing but being too tired, or (it could have been) too frightened to cry, still—whatever— evidently the child had not been found till long, long after his family, fleeing away from him in purposeful intention of drawing off the pursuers, had been found. Perhaps might not have been found at all, were it not for the toy, key to the questing Volanth as well as, now, to the Tarnisi.

The levy-lord's voice was deceptively low and thin. "The boy's blood hasn't quite dried yet," he said. "The apes may not have reached their holes yet. Let's—"

Cominthal's voice cut in. "We'll bury them, I must hope," he said, not so much asking as threatening. "They deserve that, even though only lacklanders."

"We don't know what or who—"

"They were lacklanders! Who doesn't know that landed folk never need live near Volanth!"

The levy-lord made a swift gesture. Five men—less would have been in danger—were detailed to attend to the quick sepulture; the rest skimmed on. And on. And on. The line changed formation often, according to the terrain and possible traces seen; during one such maneuver Tonorosant came close enough to Hob Tellecest for them to exchange glances. The latter was first to look away; he was pale, and his face twitched. It was doubtful that he had had the prophylactic experience of growing up in Pemath Old Port. And then the hundred spread out into wings again and Tonorosant lost sight of him. He found that he pitied the younger man: Surely it was not for this that he had parted with his own likeness, his own past folded up and laid on the shelf like a garment. No one, in foreign parts, dreaming envious dreams of Tarnis the rich, romance, would have ever included any of this in his fancy, in his visions.

They found the burnt-out shell of the house the dead had fled from while still quick. All the animals had been butchered, not skillfully, and the stench of them lay heavy upon the bitter smell of the burning, like the stench of rotten fish. Here the murdered man had lived in some small state, checking on the coming and going of the aborigines, administering the dilute law of the marches. Listening to his wife's, his mother's complaints, playing, probably, certainly, with his child. Half-glad, no doubt, of having to keep up no pretense; half—no: more, assuredly, much more than merely half-bitter at having no such true state as would need no pretense. A life less rich than any in the settled lands below led, but perhaps not much if at all a less honest one; certainly a more useful one.

At any rate, at least a placid life. Conceive, then, the sudden terror, the sort that first swells—then wrenches—then freezes the heart, when the world split open and the fire leaped out. The frantic grabbings-up of this and that, the dash for life, the searing decision to conceal the child and flee away from him in hopes of perhaps returning shortly, or—if the naked face of truth dared even then be looked upon —the knowledge that they would never see him again, only the hope that rescue might be for him at least in time . . .
. . . which it was not. . . .

* * *

The sunset sky had turned palest, dimmest yellow when they reached the beginnings of the trees, the heavy and twisted trunks from which the resinous gums were extracted, the leaner ones which produced the exquisite fruits, the straight and tall-timber trees; and there on the skyline lay Compound Ten, their destination. Here the Pemathi clerks came in season to trade and purchase, tally taxes, assemble and pack commodities, and all the other detailed things which their employers found so boring.

But before they could more than notice, fleetingly, another hundred skimming down in the distance, making for the rude comfort which lay within the compound's walls, a man toppled from his float and fell, turning, to the ground. He had fallen silently; the next one cried out, the third struggled for balance as he screamed; then all crouched and sought for altitude and now the noise was all from below and two of the masterless craft crashed in gouts of steam and one smashed into another just behind it and the Volanth bayed and howled and leaped as though they had chance to catch those making the swift-flying shadows—

And still their stones thudded and flew, thicker than the flight of startled birds which added their cries to the confusion.

Confusion, though, not for long; for now the floats rallied, they wheeled and swooped, fire-charges cracked and crackled and fumed, the grasses burst into flame. Tonorosant saw the tangle-haired- and snaggle-beard-framed faces, the mouths distended with inarticulate shoutings and wordless hootings, the long hairy arms scooping low and coming up and flinging, so fast, so swift, they seemed almost to whirl. . . . He could smell the filthy, bitter, raw, male-musty animal smell of them; smell as (it seemed) alive with brute rage as the sound of them. He swiveled, sighted, fired his charge, saw face blacken, thought of the blackened body of the Volanth woman in the swamp; swerved and went up and went away, they all went up and away, the howling was feebler and fewer there below and behind them in the burning grass as the levy-hundred sped at top speed for the shelter of Compound Ten—

And, he saw, in the waning, lemon-pale light, there were fewer in the sky, now, as well.

He had a sudden flaring-up fear, but neither then nor later, nor later yet at the levy-muster within the compound grounds, did he see anything nor did he hear anything of his so newly-found, so briefly-held, so little-known friend (but only then and at first and at last realizing him for a friend: too late), the "returned exile," Hob Tellecest.

Too late. Too late. Too late.

And, early as they were all up and out that next morning, and quickly as they found him: still too late. Forever too late.

"If we were to wash them with soap for a thousand years," one grizzle-haired lord declared, "they would still be filthy. If we were to teach them and teach them for a thousand years, they would still be ignorant. We have tried to give them a civilized example for a thousand years . . . and they still do—this," he pointed with his chin.

Tonorosant had hoped that Tellecest might have been dead before the Volanth took him. This hope had pressed against his heart, as he came up to the group around the body, till it seemed it would force the heart out through the throat. That hope died as soon as he saw the face. There wasn't much of it left, but it was impossible to look at it and not believe that every single inflicted outrage and agony had been received in full consciousness. What had the young man and young mind inside that riven skin fled from, that could have been a tiny fraction as bad as this? And to this, then, to *this*—pulpy, bloody flesh, cracked and protruding bones, shredded by tooth and claw and sharpened stick and stone —had come the glorious dreams of Tarnis. What price, then, the Craftsmen's price, compared to this price?

As though reading, though not successfully, his present thoughts, Cominthal repeated his question of the day before. "What do you think of all this, *now*?" he asked.

The grizzle-haired lord interposed. "What should be thought by anyone?" he asked. "Only that the thing which does this must be wiped out before it does it again. Cover that—cover and place it in the decent earth, my mother's kin, lest the skies, seeing it, fall down upon us all in outrage and in wrath. . . . And then—to work. All of us. To work."

"Work," of course, was planning the campaign. It did seem to Tonorosant, though, that neither outrage nor wrath was the dominant emotion among those Tarnisi present there in wide-walled Compound Ten. "Excitement" was more like the just word, much more like it. He wondered if it were always so, in time of war. He did not know. He did suppose, though, that he would learn.

Yesterday the birds had fled, shrieking; today they perched unconcerned on trees and eaves and walls, chattering lazily to one another, now and then allowing their casual droppings to fall upon the stained ground and grass. The blood of life and all its lusts and humors had coursed through the veins of Tellecest. The alterations of his body had not altered that a bit. And now all was stopped and was forever still and all that was left in this world lay beneath the ground and grass and the wild birds of heavens let fall their filth upon it, and did not even know that it was there.

Had he, too, come here with secret, subtle plans, seeking more than just a pleasant place to hide? Did he intend something like the making and amassing of money, some day to buy his own island, too?—to share dominion over men and fields and trees with the sun and the sea, a king in minor? What had he ever done to the Volanth, that the Volanth would be justified in doing this to him? What *could* he have ever done, what could any man have ever done to any other man, that would have justified it? But none of these thoughts, of course, had the Tarnisi in common with him now, Tonorosant. They talked excitedly as the relief maps were lifted up, and in the tone and tenor of the common voice, the cast of countenance of the common face, he could find a parallel only in his recollection of the days when he and his men, down and away on the south shore of the Inner Sea of Pemath, were getting ready to go out at night to "tap"—intercept, cut, carry off—a tow of cargo. Morality had hardly been involved there, and it hardly now seemed involved here.

The levy-lord of his own hundred was named Losacamant, a small man who never seemed to smile, and who moved with an almost liquid grace of movement. In charge of the second hundred was Lord Mialagoth, he of the grizzled hair and heavy brows. The third charge-of-levy was the young and comely Lord Tilionoth, as intent upon the maps as though they were targets to cast his spears upon, but now not so self-contained, speaking to those who hovered close about him, but never taking his eyes away from the reliefs however animated his comments. Silent Pemathi upheld the great charts. One of their number, too, had been killed with great cruelty; presumably they had made their own arrangements about the body; certainly no one else had concerned himself in the matter.

"We all know how the apes act," Lord Mialagoth was saying. "It's their way to run wild, tear up whatever . . . whoever, alas, I must say . . . they come across—then they run and hide and gloat and work up their filthy courage for another attack. Last night some of us—your hundred, Lord Losacamant—bad luck—got the crest of the second wave. We have to move, move quickly, and hit them before they start up again. Now, here's the terrain; can you all see?"

He pointed to the place where the house of the deputy march warden had stood, the fatal route along which the family and their servant had fled. The long, peeled withe he was using for pointer swept up along the direction to Compound Ten, paused—pale and accusing. "Here's the ridge where the attack was made late last evening. And here *we* are." The pointer withdrew, hovered, made an arc to the east. "Here is where we are going—the apes are thickest in this direction, and we will make a fine harvest, I must hope," the addition of the formal, polite phrase coming somewhat oddly in the midst of the spare, direct language he was using. He went on to arrange with the two other levy-lords how the three hundreds were to be deployed, how signals and other communications, supplies, medical attention, and other essential but (to the Tarnisi) essentially boring matters were to be arranged. The arrangements consisted largely of leaving all such non-combatant duties to a Pemathi servants' levy, as was customary.

Later, for a long time later, the events of the campaign seldom left Tonorosant's mind. He had only to close his eyes at night to see them once again unfold, unroll, unravel, unreel. Until the time came when something screamed and seemed to batter on his mind with bloody fists, crying out, *I am not Tonorosant! I am Jerred Northi! These things did not happen to me! I will not think of them and I will not have them thought!* Night vision became nightmare, and the man who lay sweating and struggling, the man with two minds and two memories, dreamt that he awoke to find himself Jerred Northi and only him once more—in body as well. At this point, though with slow, dreadful difficulty, as one who extricates himself from a fearful grip, he forced himself fully, really awake. He lay there, composing his mind. It was better, he concluded—far better—to dream of undesired things which yet had been, than of things which could not be—

—yet.

The concave shells of the floats were bobbing gently as they got aboard, bright and scarlet shells, humming faintly with the great power of their incredibly small steam motors

—a concession to foreign technology which no Tarnisi had ever been known to oppose.

"Keep those shields full up," Lord Losacamant warned. "We won't need that much speed for the wind resistance to make that much difference—in fact: too much speed, and we'll do nothing but overshoot our marks. We haven't come all this way to do that. This hundred will keep my words in mind, I must hope."

Line after line, group after group, hundred after hundred mounted up to the designated altitude, then moved off in different directions to the assembly coordinates. And there they hovered, three great, long lines of them, drawn up in one great triangle. Then they dropped. Then they began to move. An observer, strategically situated, would have seen the scarlet triangle drawing in, inwards, ever in upon itself, diminishing in area. Those upon the ground probably would not have noticed the geometrical niceties of the arrangement: how the lines grew tighter as they grew shorter, the spaces between each craft forever diminishing. Those upon the ground had never heard of geometry, had probably never so much as traced a rough triangle with a stick in the rough dust. All that they saw and heard, all that they could know, was that punishment was soaring through the sky.

That death was coming through the sky.

At length the time came and the signal was given and the lines ceased their absolute and supra-humanly beautiful rigidity (". . . beauty bare . . . ," some ancient one had called geometry). Within no limits other than his own safety and that of his fellows, each floater was now free to do that which had brought him here. The stones thudded, the rocks rattled, all as before; as before, the voices howled— But no more than that was as before. There was no element of surprise now, and, besides, the shields were up. The Volanth fled, they ran for their lives, they sped along the ground, they leaped and bounded along for all the world as though they did not know that there was nowhere to go.

"Hold fire; contact only," was the signal for the first phase.

Contact! A delicately understated word. . . . There was here, too, a matter of mathematically calculable precision —arithmetic, though, and not geometry. When a vehicle of weight X, going at speed Y, is brought into contact with a man, the effect is as though the said man has fallen from a height of distance Z.

Perhaps, thought Tonorosant, in some idle, theorizing

corner of his mind, perhaps the word was not after all arithmetic, but algebra.

The first Volanth was flung away from his float as though an electric shock had passed through his body, hairy arms and legs flailing. The second seemed to have been badly put together and at once fell apart. The third turned and ran at him with inward-scooping arms and bared teeth—that face was visible long after nothing else of its body was. The fourth burst and smeared. The fifth—

But Tonorosant kept no more count.

In the scrub and brush and salt weeds along the Gulf of Lare, one of the few areas of Pemath which could not be and was not kept under intensive cultivation, lived the tufty, ill-tasting and ill-smelling small sandloper. Ordinarily, its flesh could not be sold for a ticky at a beggar's mart. But years came, and the man known as Jerred Northi could remember one of them, when the hunger was so great upon the land of Pemath that the poorest of the poor fled from their hovels in hordes and made for the wastelands; swarming across them and driving the sandlopers from their stinking dens and clubbing them to death—falling upon them, eating their flesh raw and bloody.

It seemed to him that this was what was happening now.

He kept trying to remember the torn body of the border warden and wife and mother. He remembered without trying the Volanth servant woman who had winked with her dead eyes. He did not want to remember the dead child . . . but he did. He did.

The morning was one great scream and smear of blood.

Suddenly the signal, *Desist*, came. It was repeated twice. Finally it was obeyed. Tonorosant found that he was sweeping around in wobbling, irregular circles. There was a droning sound in his ears and a dreadful face, dreadfully accusing, before his eyes. For a moment he thought it was the man he had ridden down, the third one, who had turned as though to fight. Then he saw that it was only part of a face. Tellecest's. "Yes," he said. And, "Thank you." The face vanished. He looked about and saw that most of the craft had grounded. There were no more signals, so, after a while, he did the same.

Some of the Volanth were still running, still screaming. But the sound had a different quality now. He saw a man from his hundred walk casually over to a child who was standing there, dazed and slack-mouthed, and chop at its neck with the edge of his hand. The child went down, kicked once with one leg, moved no more. Almost at once another child sprang up from the ground and ran off, grotesquely spraddle-legged, and urinating in terror. The man did not follow, but, catching his fellow levy-man's eye, cocked his head after the fleeing, spraying child, and grinned. Then he yawned, stretched, made faces of mock deprecation. A look of great interest came suddenly upon him, and Tonorosant turned to see.

More Volanth. Running. All running. Behind them, Tarnisi. Also running. Running after the Volanth. It took a moment for him to realize that this was but a third judgement, that his first look had told him only that there were *people* running, his second thought was that some were smooth and some were hairy. Something seemed to be wrong with his mind, his thoughts were not proceeding smoothly as though on a film; they were clicking on and off, abruptly, as though on slides. *Click.* People running. *Click.* Hairy. Smooth. *Click.* Tarnisi pursuing Volanth. Proper order of things. *Click.* Something odd, *not* proper. *Click.* Man ahead looks familiar. *Click.* Lord Tilionoth. *Unfamiliar. What?*

The young lord reached out and seized one of the Volanth. They stumbled, both, were a moment upright, wrestling; tangled limbs; they fell, both, continued wrestling, tangled limbs: hairy ones, smooth ones: making dreadful noises, both of them. Then the figure pinned beneath, the Volanth, ceased to struggle. But the one on top did not. *What?*

Click.

Man. Woman.

Click. . . .

And the man from Tonorosant's hundred, who had been watching with intense, involved excitement, making encouraging, unconscious sounds, suddenly gave an abrupt cry which was almost a groan. Slipped from his clothes. Was gone, running, running, shouting.

Running, shouting, running, running, he was running in the hot, still air, and the hideously frightening and unfamiliar noises were behind him and beside him and ahead of him and his head hurt his legs hurt his feet hurt, he dared not stumble, he turned aside, there was no background and no scenery, and he ran and he ran and he ran—

Again Tonorosant stepped forward, took command, and again Jerred Northi and Jerred Northi's memories of Pemath were subdued and sank away. A bird sang, briefly, overhead.

He cursed it. It was life, and life was loathsome. What use was it to flee from Pemath, child-hunt-tolerating Pemath, catering to the most corrupt tastes of the most corrupt rich —what use?—if all one's efforts accomplished nothing more than this: to find in Tarnis, golden dream: this, this, *this?*

Weakness and despair took him and shook him. He reached out for supports which were not there. It was a black moment, long and bitter and sick. It did not vanish away with a click, either, but it ebbed away, slowly, like water ebbs away into wet sand. He looked up and he blinked. Life was life. It need not be loathsome for long. And, certainly, it was better than death. Parallel lines might meet in infinity, he did not know, he had never been there to see. But sure it was that they never met before then. The parallels which only a moment before had so disturbed his mind and body were no parallels at all. Those hunted in Pemath had sinned in nothing, neither by commission nor by association. It was quite different here in Tarnis. This was a case of evil returned for evil. Nor could one nor need one nor for that matter should one be moralistic to the extent of describing this as evil. It was a mere matter of simple fact that on the present occasion the Volanth had struck the first blow, committed the first killing, the first rape, the first child-murder. And as for any question of who had struck the first blow over a thousand legend-shrouded years ago, what could be more futile than trying to follow such a trail. Probably no one and yet everyone.

He sighed. Like Pemath, Tarnis had a curse upon it. But he had needed not remain forever in Pemath. And nor need he here.

* * *

Long lines of sweating Volanth staggering beneath poled bales and baskets filed into Compound Ten, set down their burdens at direction of the drab-capped and -kilted clerks. The stores were being piled in steps and by now some of the steps had already been filled in solidly up to the tops of the compound's walls. Timber and resin and grain, edible seeds and stables and sun-dried fruit, packed and sacked, root crops and dried fish, herbs and bark, and other items for which Tonorosant had no names. Most of the levy-men milled about, talking excitedly, giving the burdens and their bearers no more than an indifferent glance. One, however, went up to the tally-man.

"There's more food-chop down there in the mud granaries along the ridge," he said, gesturing.

The tally-man made a precise tick on his chart, gestured a gasping porter to halt. "Yes, master. We know. We not go-take it."

"No? Oh. Why not, boy?"

The Pemathi gave a very slight shrug of his neat shoulders. "If we go-take all food-chop, master, tese Volant go-starve."

"Let them!"

"If tey go-starve, master, be nobody go-grow food-chop here, next year."

The Tarnisi, grown bored even before the answer was finished, turned and walked away. The tally-man made another tick on his chart, looked up, spat neatly in the middle of the porter's face, gestured him onward, and brought his withe down in a stinging blow across the bent, retreating back. Then he beckoned the next one forward.

Tonorosant moved about, looking, listening. Lord Tilionoth was the center of a little group, all of whom were smiling. "No, really, did I take the first dip this morning?" he asked. "No one was in before me? Well, well . . . ." He preened himself. "I got in twice more, after that, you know—" There was laughter.

"Here we do our best," an older man said—grizzled Lord Mialagoth, "to keep their numbers down . . . and young lusty sprigs like my brother's son here do *their* best to keep the numbers *up!*" There was more laughter.

Tilionoth said, with shy determination, "And if we can get together after lunch, I will get in twice more or so, I must hope."

Another burst of merriment. "—spearsman in more senses than one," Mialagoth guffawed.

"One grows tired of it, you know," the young man went on, "if it becomes just a matter of rolling over in bed for it. But when a man has to run and wrestle for it—eh? You see what I mean. *Well*. I hope lunch isn't long delayed. This whole campaign has given me the keenest appetite I've had in years. One should really be very *grate*ful to the Volanth . . . wouldn't you agree?"

They smiled and chuckled and nodded, and they patted him on the back.

CHAPTER SIX

Tonorosant had never been so active as now, after his return to the inlands. He swam, furiously and alone, hour after hour, in the cold and misty dawn alike as in the heat of noon. He spent long successive days checking and rechecking every detail of business with his clerks. He skimmed and darted and sped up and down the waterways, sometimes avoiding by none too safe a margin the nets and the weirs of the squat, sullen River Volanth. At night, often exhausted, but never, never pleasantly weary, he took the aids of drugs to help him sleep. They did not banish his dreams, they made them dimmer, and in the mornings he could remember only that they had not at all been nice.

But from people in general he remained away as much as he was able. The elegant young men, now laughing, now languid, so proud of their sleek and supple limbs and all the skills they had with them—these young men now aroused in him no longer any feelings of friendship, but only of disgust. He avoided the contacts which had previously served both friendship and commerce. Curiously—or, perhaps, not at all curiously—this seemed to arouse no hostility. On the contrary.

Lord Losacamant's wife visited him, ostensibly to inquire if a "foreign toy" in which an older grandchild had expressed interest, was really both safe and proper. If this was her real reason or not, the mission was one which gave little good excuse to linger. She looked at her host, as he saw her out, with interest and sympathy.

"Poor young man," she said, "he looks both sad and drawn. Ah, in your lonely exile you thought little, I must hope, that life among your own people could bring such sharp pain."

"Lady Losacamant is very kind. I shall look happier another time, I must hope."

"And I. You have seen dreadful things . . . . Well. They won't occur often enough for you to grow used to them, I must hope, but may it not be that memory will fade? Come and see us at your convenient pleasure. We have old, sunken

71

gardens which have, and have deserved some fame. I shall show you around. You will plan on it, I must hope . . . . I have many charming granddaughters," she added, a trace of a smile stirring the composure of her mouth.

Another visitor, and, to Tonorosant's subsequent surprise, one who to turned out to be not long unwelcome, was grayhaired Guardian Othofarinal. He had come to remind him of his former agreement to interest himself on behalf of the returned exiles.

"Unless action is taken, and firmly, and soon, they may in large measure merely augment the lackland class . . . which is, my sister's sib, already large enough; in fact, over-large."

Something flashed through Tonorosant's mind and was evidently reflected on his face, however fleeting-fast, for the Guardian leaned forward and looked at him, keenly.

"You have already had some thoughts upon that subject, then, I take it? I would hear. I would hear."

He hesitated. Then, slowly, and without mentioning a name, he recounted the incident of the lacklander in the levy at the time of the outland campaign: first, his distinctive type of unpleasantness; and, next, his resentment at the possibility of its being perhaps thought not essential to bury the desecrated bodies because they might have been lacklanders. Othofarinal nodded.

"Their resentment is perhaps only too well-founded and of too long standing, although it is often based upon trifles, or, indeed, upon nothing at all. And it is also true that their near-poverty is usually the reason for their accepting of positions which no one else would want. That murdered warden up there in the Outlands was undoubtedly happier and—until the end—better off than he would have been back here among us; still, though I never knew him, I'm in no doubt that he also resented his being there every single day, intensely and bitterly.

"What is to be done for them? The Lords, surely, will do nothing. It is a basic principle of theirs that, if anything should have been done about a particular thing, it would already have been done; since nothing was done about it, nothing *should* be done about it. So we see a class on whom the burdens of aristocracy are pressed and at the same time deprived of the means of maintaining that burden. *Lacklanders*. Why need they lack land? There is land enough for all . . . .

"More sons of the exiles are returning from abroad in

these days than in any others. This is, basically, a good thing. It was a bad thing that anyone ever went into exile at all. But the good may be swallowed up in the bad if provision for them—other than the personal kindnesses of individuals—continues to be not made. I do not necessarily say—*necessarily*, mind you—that an estate ought to be taken away from a family which has occupied and enjoyed it for two generations, and given to a returned exile whose family had it until two generations ago. Moreover, heirships are often matters of dispute, people often lack documents, not seldom they have only vague notions or sometimes none at all of who, precisely, their forebears were. Nor is it of signal consequence. Do they have the Seven Signs? They do? Enough."

The older man grew free and eloquent. Now and then he very softly beat the cushions of his palms gently for emphasis. There were, for example, he pointed out, the idle lands, lands which had escheated to the governance for a variety of non-political reasons. Why should not division and choice be made among those for the benefit of, on the one hand, the older, lackland class; and, on the other, the newer, returned exile class?

"It would provide them with funds and income, basic essentials. It would give them interests, lawful and proper interests. Occupation. How can it be gainsaid that a dissatisfied portion of the populace is a dangerous portion of it?

"And there are other possibilities, too. Why might not new lands be opened up? There are legions of leagues of them, where nothing human moves or has ever moved—not even Volanth! Yes, yes: Ah, there's no shortage of possibilities. The thing is to make a beginning, and in order to do *that* we must make a decision. The Guardians cannot do it alone, you know. Nor could the Lords—assembled or otherwise—not that they would want to. All the elements of governance must be together in this, and the only way to assure that is to make it plain and public that elements outside of the governance are determined. They should be. So I have come to you. So I have come *again* to you. Begin to act. You must do so and you will do so, I must hope."

So began another sort of work in which to immerse himself. Involved in factionalism and intrigue? He shrugged the thought away. It was perhaps possible that the Guardians were no better than the Lords, but that, too, was worth no more than a shrug. He would distract his mind until, at last, it needed no further distraction; and he would entrench his position here until its roots and its strength went as deep into Tarnisi life as they could go.

Atoral had ceased to come to see him because of his sullenness and coldness during his most moody period. He did not, could not blame her. But now he felt that it was time for him to go to her.

He found her in the golden garden of her small town house; an old-fashioned custom or conceit which she cherished: to have a garden consisting in only plants whose leaves or flowers were gold-colored, so chosen and so situated that the tint stayed dominant in the area in every season of the year. She came up to him gravely but not reproachfully and put her fingers on his hands as she had done that first time and she said, "You will stay some little while with us at least, I must hope." He took her hands in his and then held her in a light embrace, but did not kiss her.

They walked in slow silence up the shallow steps furred in golden moss, under the branches of trees from which little leaves dropped like a golden rain; they walked back again through the golden buds and golden blossoms, and thus, back and forth and to and fro, he managed to tell her something of the deep, frozen hate and horror which had come upon his heart. "They say, you—all of you—you always say, the Volanth are like animals. And I've seen how they can be, and I know it. But I've seen the Tarnisi like animals as well. And so I see nothing to choose between them, and it's made all this land I longed so long for, it's made it abhorrent and abominable to me."

She murmured, "Oh, not all of it, not all of us, I must hope."

With fiercely twisted face thrust suddenly so close to hers —but she did not flinch nor turn aside—he said, "I couldn't stand to have you near me because it makes me think of your flesh and my flesh—together—and I could not dare to do that and to think of what I saw of flesh and flesh—" His voice choked. It was as though blood had choked it. And they turned in unspoken consent and they walked again in silence, up and down the golden walks and through the golden shrubbery, until, at last, he knew (and knew she did, too), that he was healed as well as he might hope to be; knew, too, that this was healed enough.

For more than that he might never hope to be healed,

unless he was healed of life itself, "that disease whose only cure is death."

* * *

Now, with his mind so much more at ease, and his position as at least symbolic, representative, of the returned exiles more firm, Tonorosant had time to look around and into other matters.

Lady Losacamant had been guilty of not even pardonable exaggeration when she said that she had "charming granddaughters." There were three of them, lovely as newly blossoming flowers, and not less lovely were the famous sunken gardens which they graced—though, "lovely" was perhaps too light a word to describe the gardens' grace and dignity; handsome, they were; rather, even than beautiful. The aery trickery of the golden gardens seemed, in comparison, to be transient and insubstantial—and merely pretty.

At length their grandfather himself, the spare-of-words Lord Losacamant, appeared upon the scene, as Tonorosant had known he would. He greeted the girls with a grave though affectionate gesture, and to his guest was courteous without being curious. There was, after all, not very much of the curious in the visit. They were neighbors of no great distance, the lady had specifically invited him to adventure hither, and if the girls were still a shade too young to be taking lovers, why, they would not be so always or forever. And it might also be said that the two men were or had been comrades-in-arms. Officer and follower.

His lordliness dismissed the girls to their grandmother, who gracefully though nonetheless promptly withdrew with them to the house. Host and guest regarded one another a moment. However reasonable the reasons which Tonorosant had given in his own mind as not only justifying his visit but making it close to commonplace, he could now no longer believe that Losacamant believed in one of them, even for a single moment. There was no challenge in the calm look the lord gave his visitor, nothing of derision or displeasure. It did not even estimate. It did not even announce. It merely let it be known.

The massive blocks of stone which formed the walls of this part of the sunken gardens dripped with moisture which cooled the air as well as nourishing the infinity of green and flowering plants set between them. The turf was both firm and springy. Overhead a palisade of heavy grasses thick as thin saplings arched inward. It was gratefully dim and cool.

Looking at his host's characteristic walk, which seemed to pronounce without any degree of boasting the existence of the small but muscular body concealed within the robes, Tonorosant wondered if this were typical or merely peculiar —and if the former, if some lesson were not therein embodied.

"My former interests," he said, at last, after Losacamant had made some polite reference to the subject, "have seemed of less concern and importance to me of late. I think you may understand why, my father's kin."

The levy-lord nodded, unsurprised. "Life among foreigners had not prepared you," he said, "for the facts of war. Although they also lack the Seven Signs, they cannot be compared to those who lack them here . . . not in all respects."

"Can nothing be done about the Volanth?"

Losacamant's eyebrows rose very slightly. "You saw what was done. 'Nothing?' "

"Nothing to prevent its happening again . . . ?"

"Ah. 'Again.' How? A Volanth no more recalls last year than a bird does last week."

"Then you say, in effect: 'No. Nothing.' "

A slight cant of the head, a slight move of the hand. "Destroy them? It has sometimes been counseled." He seemed to consider it all over again, and, after a long moment, said, "No." Another long moment passed. "However . . . ."

"Yes, august lord?"

"Since you show interest—and it pleases me that you do —the matter is not unimportant . . . . Go and see my lord Mialagoth. He will have useful words for you, I must hope." They turned and walked up slowly from the sunken gardens to where the sun was bright and warm.

* * *

Lord Mialagoth's brows were black and bushy, with here and there a long white hair writhing indignantly—or so it seemed. "What puzzles you?" he asked.

"For one thing, that no particular effort was made to discover the actual murderers of the march warden's family."

"What was there to discover? Who could they have been? Tarnisi? Lermencasi? Pemathi? Bahon? They were Volanth!

None but Volanth act like that. None but Volanth were there to act at all."

Tonorosant saw his point, which had seemed so clear to him, escaping, and he tried hard not to let it do so. "Agreed, then, my mother's uncle, that the murderers were Volanth. I must ask, *which* Volanth? How can we be sure that the ones who committed the actual murder are not still alive?"

Something like a faint spasm passed over the face of Lord Mialagoth. Here he had been, painting leaves at his easel, a task requiring the utmost subtlety—and then came this unsought visitor with his exceedingly unsubtle and intrusive questions. With a brief sigh he lay down his brush. "The best of the light has passed. I will paint no more today." He rose and faced Tonorosant. "It seems to me that you are suggesting that we proceed as though we are police. I know that they are much concerned with police matters in foreign parts, but it is not our way in Tarnis. I say this not to reproach you, not at all. I say it to make you understand that I do understand your concern. But . . . .

"Here at Manyponds we have ornamental orchards which were originally set out by my great-grandfather. I have seen it fail but seldom that, just as the fruits begin to ripen, certain birds come and try to feed upon them. Now. My daughter's son. *It is of no concern to me whatsoever which birds were guilty*. It is in the nature of birds that they try to steal fruit. If ten succeed in doing it today, ten hundred will attempt it tomorrow. Don't you see?"

"I do. Exactly. So—"

"So I do not bother directing my steward, 'Discover the guilty birds.' I direct him: 'Drive away the birds. All of them. Every one of them.'"

"But—"

"'But how?' you are about to ask. At one time we did it afoot, with swords and spears. Now we use more modern methods, although admittedly dependent upon foreign-made devices. I have never been one of those who felt obligated to employ only classical ways in all things. What are the classical ways to those who lack the Seven Signs? If you can think of more effective methods in dealing with the matter, we will all be obliged to you, I must hope."

* * *

So much, then, for the "useful words" of Lord Mialagoth. Of the levy-lords, only Tilionoth was left. Tonorosant found him in his kennels, with sleeves rolled up, directing the preparation of his dogs' dinner.

"Can you conceive of it, my brother's brother," he said to his guest, "that for three whole days the new kennelman had been feeding them raw eggs? *Raw eggs!* And so now I must direct him in the proper fashion myself. Boil them with a small handful of salt, cool them slowly under cool, running water. Thus the shells come off smoothly, easily, leaving no fragments behind. Then cut them into eight pieces—no more and no less. Add pieces of boiled liver of the same size exactly, four parts of liver to one of eggs. Add to this a fifth part of plain bread, also broken up to the same size, crumb as well as crust. Now mix them slowly . . . slowly. . . ." He dipped his hands into the mixture and turned it about. ". . . slowly. Just that way. It is not difficult. Now—

"Is the broth ready? Let me have it." He dipped in a finger, nodded his content at the temperature, tasted, nodded again. "Now, see how I pour it . . . slowly . . . slowly. . . . And now allow it to sit for exactly a quarter of an hour, do you understand? In the meanwhile—"

In the meanwhile they went to visit the dogs, alert and happy animals with long, smooth blue-gray coats, obviously overjoyed to see their master. He greeted them all by name, explained the personalities and good qualities of each, until presently it was time for their dinner, and the kennelman —somewhat subdued, still, by his gaffe in the matter of the eggs—appeared to call them thereto.

"You will stay for our own dinner, I must hope," Tilionoth said. "I am alone tonight. She has gone to her parents. That is well, of course, that she should do so; still, I feel her absence. It has been quite well with us," he said, contentedly —then, courtesy rising above the pleasure of personal reminiscence, he said, "But you will not think that this is the only reason (my loneliness) that I ask you, I must hope. There is so much we might talk about. . . . I have been pleased to hear of your close connection with the right people. You will have heard that my being of the Lords does not obscure my basic attachment to the Guardians." He let his hand rest lightly upon his guest's shoulder. Tonorosant murmured the polite and proper phrases. With some effort, he managed not to think too much of the last occasion on which he had seen Lord Tilionoth, or of what he had seen him doing.

After that dinner, almost elaborate in its simplicity,

Tonorosant turned the talk in the direction he desired. It was not difficult, the host was no complex person. "Ah, the Volanth," he said. He reached for a piece of fruit. He ate it. He wiped his fingers. Evidently he felt that he had made what was for the moment at least a sufficient comment.

Tonorosant pressed ahead. "What do you think of the proposition which I am told is made from time to time that the frequent campaigns against the Volanth are wasteful of time and life and effort?—and that some other method should be found—"

Lord Tilionoth had begun to shake his head even before the question was more than half-asked. "Tarolioth and his little clique," he said, interrupting. Then a light flush of embarrassment stained his handsome face a moment, and he bit at his full lips. "You will pardon my speaking of them as though in contempt, I must hope," he went on. "I had for the moment forgotten that you are the known lover of his younger daughter. Though I must disagree with them entirely, it does not excuse my speaking or seeming to speak in improper terms."

Tonorosant covered his surprise by merely bowing as though to indicate that forgiveness was not needed but was nonetheless extended. It seemed the right time to say no more but wait and hear what the other would say.

"Tarolioth and those who agree with him," the young lord continued, having cleared his throat, "are always talking about using more effective methods to civilize the Volanth. Keep them peaceful. And so, no violence. Well—

"All very pleasant for the *Volanth,* I agree. But what of *us?*"

He said the last word with such triumphant emphasis that his guest felt he had to break silence . . . though only with a noncommittal syllable into which the young man evidently read approval, for, "Do you see," he swept on, making it a declarative and not a question.

"What of the Tarnisi? Surely it is our interests which must be predominate! Tarolioth's views are totally unrealistic, he and his friends seem unaware of how weak and how effete our culture would be without these outlets. It's been centuries since there has been real, full-scale war with the Volanth, and in that period—despite the time so many of us put in our estates—we have become an urbanized civilization, and such are always subject to decadence and softening due to the absence of conflict." He spoke so swiftly and glibly that his listener had the feeling he was hearing the views of another, or of others, which had been often repeated until accepted as true faith.

"Do not think at all, you will not at all think, I must hope, that I am speaking slightily of the classcial ways when I say that such things as painting leaves form an insufficient stimulus. And even things like spear-throwing, of which I am myself so fond, as you may know, are purely artificial in the present state of civilization. Life becomes bland, it becomes boring, we find some outlet in those foreign toys which you are kind enough. . . . But it is not enough! It is not enough!

"We require the opportunity to risk our lives, and to risk them in combat. We must have an outlet against—what is the word?—*surfeit!* Yes.—To stir up our blood—even if we may have to shed it! That is why I have said that we must be grateful to those Volanth brutes for giving us the excuse. And we cannot, no, we cannot dispense with it. Do you see?"

Tonorosant thought that he did. He thought that he saw, perhaps, too much. . . . Tilionoth, complaining that he had grown tired of sex when it had become "just a matter of rolling over in bed for it"; Tilionoth, stripped to his skin, pursuing the women of the Volanth—not once and again, but again and again; and then, just now before dinner, remarking complacently about his lady-lover that it had "been quite well with" them. . . .

Tonorosant bowed again, deeper than before, to hide his face.

"Furthermore, though of course it is perhaps a trivial point, I believe that even the Volanth benefit—What? Yes, I do. They do. It stirs *them* up, too. They work the better for it." But here he was vague as to details, murmured, *commerce,* in a hopeless tone, waved his hands. One could not be expected to be specific on such a subject, Lord Tilionoth indicated.

He took his departure a bit earlier than deepest courtesy allowed, but his host appeared not much disturbed by this. "I shall see you out," he said, "then drop by the kennels on my way back to assure myself that the dogs are properly bedded down for the night. One must be forever alert. Raw eggs. . . ." He shuddered.

* * *

Tulan Tarolioth, Atoral's father. One accepted one's parentage on faith; there seemed no resemblance, physical or emotional. "Sooner or later, I knew you would want to see him," she said. Then, after some long silence en route, she added, suddenly, abruptly, "He is right, of course, but it is useless! Useless!" Nor would she explain what she meant, merely pointed, once, with a sigh, to a tree along the way: a squat, shag-barked one with inedible red fruit. "Volanth's hearts," they were called. And so, breaking silence, introduced him with voice subdued, to the tiny, nervous little man who was her father.

Her father, it soon became clear, was a man obsessed. He had two or three points to make, and he made them over and over and over again, until at last Tonorosant could see them coming. He was thus not surprised to observe that Atoral's sister, after allowing a grimace of boredom and despair to convulse her face, slipped off and was seen no more. The room they were meeting in was a morass of books and papers and writing materials, from which, from time to time, the tulan produced a small pamphlet.

"Allow me to give you a copy," he would say. Or, "Now, this may interest you." And, "Ah, I see that you already— you will forgive me, I must hope." Yet, even after that: "Allow me to give you a copy. . . ."

This was a booklet on the subject of Tarnisi-Volanth relationships which Tulan Tarolioth had published. Or, to be exact, written: It had never, it seemed, been officially published. "The subject is a delicate one," he said. "We are ashamed of it. Properly so. We ought to be ashamed of it. Do not we, who have the Seven Signs, owe a duty towards those who do not? And how do we show it? By destruction of life, destruction of property." He quoted noble and ethical sentiments from classical authors, and adduced them as evidence of the wrongness of Tarnisi attitudes towards their country's aboriginal people—a use which might well have surprised their authors, who had, never, it would seem, made the same connection themselves.

Were there many Tarnisi who agreed with him? The tulan became agitated. Of course! Very many. Numbers increasing all the time, he must hope. How could it be otherwise? Was not cruelty against the most fundamental aspects of the Tarnisi character? And he named a name, and he named other names, and then he began to name names he had already named, and then he offered Tonorosant a copy of his little booklet. "This may interest you," he said.

Atoral stayed behind. Tonorosant left with a feeling of infinite sadness.

* * *

Mothiosant and Sarlamat smiled. "Yes, of course," said Hob. "I didn't expect you to find it out for yourself . . . or, at least, we didn't think that you would do it quite so soon." His smile was brief and thin, and, like that of Mothiosant, the Commercial Delegate, had nothing in it of warmth.

"You're quite right," said Hob. "Far from being appalled at these periodic incidents of Volanth brutality, the Tarnisi are pleased. I don't suppose that any one of them, this last time, for instance, ever actually said: 'It's about time for another little war to stir our sluggish blood and to revive our flagging lusts by fun and games with the hairy women; therefore we will give such orders to one of the march wardens as cannot fail to provoke the Volanth in his territory to outrage'—I'm certain it was never put quite that way. I'm equally certain that the whole tendency of their policy for a long, long time has nevertheless been just that. And of course it *was* no accident that the Tarnisi victims were lacklanders. They can always be spared, you know."

Tonorosant said, "Awful."

"Oh, yes," Mothiosant said.

"Then . . . their whole economy is based on their stealing what the Volanth produce, isn't it? Under the guise of 'punishing' them?"

"Largely, Tonorosant, yes. My inability—in my official capacity, that is—to fulfill on occasion commercial contracts I was obliged, in the same capacity, to make earlier—we allow it to be passed off as part of 'our,' Tarnisi, incapacity for coarse trade. It's usually as simple as this: they neglected to provoke an uprising in time to provide them with the goods contracted for. The resin trees, for example, were not really sick this last season at all; but we had to tell the Bahon buyers something, and were just tired of saying, 'Oh, excuse us for not being businessmen. . . .' By *we,* of course, I mean the Tarnisi.

"But there is another *we* and there is another *us.* Isn't there?"

Tonorosant took a deep breath. At last the waters were receding, to show the shape of the submerged shoal. "Yes," he said. "The Craftsmen."

CHAPTER SEVEN

Mothiosant nodded. Hob Sarlamat seemed to relax upon an inner sigh. For now, at least, pretense—if not fully gone—was going. "Yes," said Mothiosant. "The Craftsmen. And if you have had trouble, with your two faces, intending just to work and play a while and then be gone, think and consider what difficulties we have had adjusting ourselves, ostensibly, to this monstrous and appalling arrogance forever."

Hob said, softly, "Only it won't be forever. The time is coming closer. Which means it's growing shorter. And when it arrives, *Jerred Northi,* where will you be?"

It was on his lips, those full, smooth Tarnisi lips which were not really his, to say, As far away as I can possibly help it! What was to keep him here? He had paid his bill, he was making his money, things were not going to move so rapidly that he would not be able to make more before they moved too rapidly (or came to a crashing halt), and he had kept in mind the proverb of the overseas Pemathi: *"One should always have one's money in another country, but one should always be in the country where one's money is . . . ."*

It made perhaps little difference whether the island he was going to buy was a bit bigger or a bit smaller. He would not be spending all of his time on it, anyway. Orinel had more to offer his still questing heart than, probably, he would ever be able to exhaust. It made little difference to him if the Craftsmen achieved their obviously enormous aims sooner or later. And if they, or any of them, thought that they had him in a vice, they would learn that they had not. He had paid their price. They were nothing to him. They were his friends. They were his friends.

This sudden about-face of his thoughts brought, despite his control, a wordless sound to his lips. His body moved, trembled. In a rush of confusion he searched his mind for the key, found it in another proverb, a universal one and probably of immense age. *The enemy of my enemy is my friend.*

Certainly he could throw off all obligations to the Craftsmen. He had been betrayed by Tarnis, the Tarnisi had proven unworthy of his hope and love. He could pursue his selfish search for pleasure elsewhere, his inner-centered drive for personal security. And he could never forget, wherever he went or fled, whatever he did or tried to do, the bleeding and shattered bodies lying—oh, so needlessly! so very, very needlessly!—upon that Outlands hill. . . .

Rather slowly and thickly, too shattered to say much, he said, "I? I'll be where you want me to be. I'll help you."

Monstrous and appalling arrogance, yes. It had to be put down. No man could refuse to assist in that. And then, up through the waves of still tingling shock, came the recollection that not all Tarnisi had partaken of the monstrous and the appalling. There was Atoral, her father, and her father's friends. Could one leave them alone, abandon them to . . . no.

Firmly, now, and clearly, once again master of himself, he said, "There isn't any doubt that I can be of help. I want to—and I will."

Sarlamat nodded. Mothiosant seemed to swell, then, in an instant, he was as usual. And said, blandly, urbanely, "Then, indeed, all shall be as you have said, I must hope."

* * *

The more Tonorosant applied himself to the work urged on by Mothiosant, "aiding returned exiles," finding places for them which might be of key importance when the time for the overthrow came, the more he found himself involved in the affairs of the lackland class. Looking backwards, later on, it seemed that this all began about the time he began seeing so much of Cominthal. Then, however, he made no connection. He could never be quite sure that there was one, really.

The man was there one afternoon, when Tonorosant walked out onto his grounds to stretch his legs. It was impossible to say if he had just come in and paused en route to the largehouse, or if he had for some time been sightseeing. He showed neither confusion nor embarrassment, however, but merely gazed at Tonorosant with his lowering and usually sullen look, and said, "I'm doing you the courtesy of enquiring if you've suffered no ill effects from the campaign. It was a new thing for you. Sometimes people suffer. Sometimes they don't know it until a while later."

Tonorosant was surprised and, somehow, oddly touched. He expressed his thanks, invited him to return to the house. But the man, with a mumble, and elaborately polite bow which seemed as sincere as it was inexplicably grotesque, declined. And slipped away.

There was another occasion. Night, lamps reflecting forever on the river, music of the *sint* and *harn,* many people, voices near and not so near. Glitter of lights on silver shoulder crests. Fragrant woods smoldering in the fireplaces, soft-footed and soft-voiced Pemathi servants in procession, laden with trays of foods. Laughter. A moment's silence, such as falls now and then on every conversation, every gathering. And, in the silence, a voice.

"To freedom!"

A man, face almost aggressive in what was immediately seen to be an immense effort to look unself-conscious, holding up his glass. Cominthal. The guests looking from one to another in polite incomprehension. The expression on Cominthal's face faltered, slipped, was replaced by one entirely different. In an entirely different voice, he said, "Oh, I'm not pwonouncing the wo'd cowwectly. You will pa'don me, I must hope. To fweedom!"

Understanding was immediate. There were scattered laughs, and here and there people held up their glasses and nodded to Cominthal as they drank. There was a patronizing note in it, the sort one assumes towards other peoples' children. Or towards those adults who show by behavior not yet offensive but ordinarily impermissible that they have had too much to drink.

One would not, sober, at a formal gathering, imitate Volanth or Quasi.

And then, after the tide of the evening had already washed away immediate recollection of the incident, Cominthal said, not boisterously, but over-loudly, "You like to swim."

Mildly puzzled, but not really curious; certainly not annoyed, Tonorosant said, "Yes."

"Yes...." Cominthal's eyes drooped a trifle as he gave the syllable a curious emphasis. "You swim much...."

"Should one not swim ... ?"

"Oh, by all means. Very healthful. Approved by the ancients." And, withal, after announcing these innocuous, acquitting phrases, Cominthal seemed to indicate, by winks and grimaces and shrugs, that there was nevertheless something oddly important and significant in the fact of Tonorosant's having gone swimming. And that, he, Cominthal, was somehow privy to it. But Tonorosant had no notion in the world at all of what he might have meant.

And again the pleasantness and business, the social commerce of the gathering, closed in upon itself and bore the host away. When he next looked up it was to be aware of Cominthal sitting quite alone and wrapped in the brooding mantle of his discontent.

Not long after that was the first of many visits from the aging woman, whom he came to think of as the Scrawny Dowager, and her three plump daughters. She brought with her a picture as clear as it was ridiculous of herself sitting at the table and helping herself to all the best pieces and then, bit by bit, and with a multitude of ostentatiously loving gestures, redistributing them all unto her daughters. Till she was left with little but a dirty plate and a vast sense of her own nobility, nourishing herself upon the belief in her own self-sacrifice and generosity, in which all three of the round, tight-skinned maidens loudly and often acquiesced. Upon her head was piled the elaborate coiffeur of the Tarnisi matron; a glance at it showed him that it was not one of his own synthetic imports, and a second glance at the subtle signs of shabbiness in the garb of mother and of daughters brought forth another image: in this one the three chicks repaid the broody hen with hours of effort setting in place the plumage there was no hired hairdresser to attend to

Settled, at last, mother and daughters, in the chairs arranged for them by the efficient Pemathi house-boy, formalities of a general nature taken care of, formalities of a more specific nature were brought forward.

"We are of the house and family of Tulan Arnosant," the Scrawny Dowager announced, with a deceptively casual air; her eyes and the eyes of her daughters meanwhile covertly darting little looks at him to see how he was taking this revelation. "About whom it is certainly not necessary to say anymore, I must hope."

He said nothing, there being nothing he could say. He had never heard of Tulan Arnosant, and the careful absence of any identifying criteria made it likely that the tulan had gone to ghostland a number of generations ago, his wraith being summoned up in the absence of any more recent titled member of house and family.

"And we have come to see what is being done about restoring our lost lands to us, it being perfectly clear even to those unfortunate to be afflicted with deficient vision, that there must be a superfluity of lands available to distribution, considering unto whom, I would be excused the grossness of naming names, lands are even now being distributed, I must hope."

At least one of the spherical daughters was aware that this last phrase was added out of optimism rather than grammatical appropriateness, but her glance went unheeded. The Scrawny Dowager had doubtless rehearsed her speech over and over, and was not to be denied. Her eyes went round and round the room as she spoke, feasting on the modestly-contrived opulence, but always and always coming back to Tonorosant and then to her daughters.

"It is not to be conceived, my cousin's cousin and dear returned young man from bitter exile," she swept on, "that a family whose lineage is well-famed and unimpeachable should be in any note or manner excluded against at, inasmuch as the facts of the unhappy tragedy are utterly on record of how Tulan Arnosant was deprived, must I not say 'robbed,' of his inheritance and although his house and family continue to this present to be deservedly prominent and without fear of blemish." She paused for breath and approbation, then went on before he could speak. "Still, all of wrong must be set right, as says the great Sohalion, as like the littlest leaf. And thus, my uncle's nephew, how does it dare to come about, how does it *dare*?"—her voice rose and broke and her poise shattered and she glared and trembled: "—that whilst we are often confused for lack of our entitles, one sees on every hand how those who are not to be named actually *prosper*? What? We with our lineage? while they have none at all, except such as is not to be mentioned, as one would fail to mention *beasts*? Oh!

"We hear from all sides how the Guardians are at last extending themselves against those wicked Lords and that you are the one person on whom everyone may depend. Therefore, my father's kith, I tell you with all the courtesy proper and forthcoming, we are here to receive justice while it is still available and before *everything* is *given away*—!"

Her voice ended on a shriek and this time she looked neither at the furnishings nor at her daughters, and Tonorosant, though he was largely baffled, believed her to be sincere.

Even if, as he thought likely, merely sincerely confused.

After she and her daughters had departed, assured of every consideration being given their claims, and bearing with them various ceremonious gifts which were not able to hurt their tender pride, Tonorosant thought a moment. —Those not to be named . . . whose lineage was that of beasts. . . . What she meant, untangled from the confusion of language intended to be elegant and to impress with a sense of her belonging to the proper strata of the aristocracy, was evidently a reference to that class which lay below (far, far below) even the lackland class.

He had his float brought out—not the scarlet one of current fashion, with its mean memories of blood and slaughter, but a gray one. It gave the faintest hisses from its tiny but powerful motor, rose on its cushion of air, and was off across the beautifully tended grounds and the broad, meandering river. This was a beautiful country, Tarnis. At least . . . its appearance was beautiful. . . .

Presently he heard himself hailed and in a moment a float of old-fashioned manner drew next to his; peering out were the bearded and benevolent features of the Sapient Laforosan.

"Where are you going, my young grandson from over the seas returned?" the old man asked.

"Greenrivers village, my father's uncle."

The sage's white brows went up, came down. His lips pursed a surprise from out the neatly-trimmed white beard. He shot a sudden, somewhat disturbed look at Tonorosant. Then his face relaxed into its customary benevolent blandness. "No. . . . You are not one of those who would further afflict those already sufficiently afflicted, I must hope."

Below, a water-wander surfaced, regarded them gravely with its large eyes, then dove again, its long tail undulating for a long second, then was quite gone; only the weeds waved in its wake.

"You refer. . . ."

"Come, my child. Greenrivers Village is known to be a center of Quasi life. Is it not?"

Tonorosant admitted this to be so. "But I assure you—you are correct in judging me favorably. I do mean them no harm. In fact, as I see that you are concerned for them, and as I suppose that you know much about them, you will assist me by accompanying me there, I must hope."

The towering turrets and sparkling roof-tops of Tarnis Town appeared presently above the parklike belt which surrounded the city. But there was little green or parklike, save for the name, in the so-called village which lay this side of the belt area. The "rivers" had become clotted with refuse, the ground was dusty and—save for more refuse—bare. The houses ranged from mere huts . . . hovels . . . caves of grass and branch . . . to more ambitious structures fabricated of scrap lumber and metal. Mangy dogs skulked and yelped, naked and half-naked children with distended stomachs and protruding navels ran about as untended as the dogs. One little dirty toddler stopped at the sight of the visitors and piddled where he stood, in sheer surprise. People swarmed about in a variety of clothes and of non-clothes. The place reeked, reminding Tonorosant of Pemath Old Port, but whereas the stench of the port was ancient in its effluvium, that of this village was raw and new. Only the smell of the people seemed the same—sweetish and sickly: the smell of poverty.

Some of the people, indeed, scowled and turned aside on seeing them. Others were abashed, looked away, peering up from lowered faces. Most, though, seemed pleased to see them, clustered up close around, shy in some cases, brash in others. And it was the people more than anything else which shocked Tonorosant.

He saw the widest variety of physical types, ranging from that which seemed identical to the Tarnisi along to that which appeared no different from the Volanth; and every conceivable graduation in between. Where had they all been? Here, of course. . . . But he had not been here. No one had mentioned it, let alone urged him to visit. He had had to find out for himself, digging and delving beneath the wall of silence: one might have thought the village to be inside a mountain the gate to which was sealed with seventeen seals, instead of open to the sun and air.

And a good thing, too, that it was: otherwise it might well be a pest house.

The old scholar spoke affably to the people, but somehow his words weren't clear to his companion; Laforosan's gestures were clear enough, though: Follow me. It afforded Tonorosant some mild, brief amusement to note that at least a few of the shacks they passed had been built largely out of the packing cases his "foreign toys" had come in. They came at last to what had evidently once been a small if conventional Tarnisi town house, though built so definitely away from the town proper. Some ragged remnants of gardens still survived, as did a few large old trees, but most of the grounds had been built over, and not recently, either, by the weathered look of the small and crowded houses. The main house was quite old, its lines tending to sag, its timbers and tiles spotted with moss, and from out the open door a man came hurrying.

He was neither young nor old and his dress was a most curious mixture: an out-of-fashion Tarnisi tunic, and a drab kilt. Laforosan spoke to him, affably, in suddenly clear Tarnisi. "Ah, my friend, may we burden you with the care of our vehicles?"

The man's face was a study in confusion. Pride was there, and gratification, and—though soon dispelled—embarrassment. For a moment he half-turned and seemed about to scurry back into the house. Then he became quite controlled, and came on forward. "Of course, the Sir Sapient. Oh, you flatter the dwelling with your visit." He said something, quick, impatient, two young men appeared from the straggle of those who had followed them or had already been there; and with smug looks stationed themselves at the now-grounded floats, imperiously gesturing everyone else away.

"This," said Laforosan, "is the noted unofficial mayor of Greenrivers village, my friend Phonorioth . . . also entitled to be known as Idón aDan. So. And this is a young returned exile who has gained and deserved much prominence, and his name is Tonorosant. You will be much taken with each other's company, I must hope."

"Yes, yes, my grandfather—" Phonorioth/Idón aDan started to say. "Oh, forgive, my bad manners, I must hope, charmed and delighted, ah, if you will permit —" He seemed eager for some reason to go on ahead of Laforosan, but the Sapient, heedless, continued his own pace. The unofficial mayor then fell back, turned, almost collided with Tonorosant, apologized again, again began to say something about his grandfather, half-attempted to dart ahead of Tonorosant, apologized, withdrew, hesitated. And thus they mounted the sunken steps and passed into the house. Tonorosant was not altogether sure of his eyes, but it did seem to him that in that first second he had seen an old, old woman crouching in front of a full-length mirror and doing something to her face. Then she turned, abruptly, looked at them with face distorted by shock and horror, turned and scuttled away on hands and knees and was gone somewhere into the inner dimness.

Tonorosant about-faced and on the face of Phonorioth he saw a mixture of shame and rage and despair. "Forgive me," he said at once, almost instinctively taking what he thought was the right line, "I fear I was inattentive to you a moment ago, my brother-in-law's brother. You will forgive me, I must hope—'your grandfather,' you were saying—?'

Every expression was washed away by gratified relief. "Yes, ah. My grandfather. . . . Pray take seats, and here, and here. I will in one moment call for a lunch to be prepared hastily and inadequately. Such as it will be, you will accept my best efforts, I must hope." They seated themselves on the old and decaying furniture and prepared to endure the burden of their host's pleasure. He sat facing them, hopped up and bowed, turned and shouted something, looked around nervously. . . . The Sapient Laforosan reached up and took a bit of his sleeve between thumb and forefinger and gently, firmly, urged him to be seated. The man beamed, relaxed a trifle.

"My grandfather was a prominent member of the mercantile aristocracy of Pemath," he launched glibly into an account which he had by rote and the telling of which gave him such pleasure that he smiled and smiled and little wet beads appeared and shone in the corners of his mouth, "who in former and more liberal times visited this country and formed a romantic liaison with a daughter of a leading house. Opposition on the part of her father, a gentleman of the old school, based upon my grandfather's foreign birth, led my grandmother to retreat here to what was then the sylvan refuge which formed part of her personal patrimony. A daughter was born of this alliance and it was my grandfather's wish that she and her mother should return with him to dwell in his ancestral mansion in the old and aristocratic Port section of Pemath City. Such, however, was my paternal grandmother's attachment to her native lands that she refused to consider this. My grandfather, thus obliged to return alone and unconsolated, perished away from insufficiently requited grief."

He gave a dramatic sigh and looked closely at Tonorosant. The latter echoed the sigh and moved his hands in an appropriate gesture. Phonorioth beamed. Part of his story, certainly, was true—the red glints in his sparse hair, the scattering of freckles, the slight but perceptible pallor of his skin—all confirmed his claim to partial Pemathi descent. Other elements of the story were of course nonsense.

"Being thus myself a child of two worlds, I have found it natural to be of what help I can to others who, though not at all of Pemathi descent," he laughed, toothily, wetly, "are in any case also of Tarnisi descent in part. Many lies will doubtless have been told you, but you will have discredited them, I must hope. For instance, the lie that the Tarnisi ancestors of the rural people of whom so many live in Greenrivers village were in ancient times cast out because of being diseased or insane. Oh, such a foul lie! Dreamed up to justify slander, oppression, injustice and scorn! Now, the truth of the matter is, that in former times there existed no barriers to inter-ethnic marriage. This is the truth of the origins of this community, so sadly mistreated."

The truth, as Tonorosant realized, was that both accounts were probably partly true and partly false. It was like enough that at one time the barriers were lower and voluntary unions had been formed. It was also like enough that outcasts for any reason from the Tarnisi community in times past had found refuge with and become part of the aboriginal nation. But what need was there to consider the remote past?— when Tonorosant well knew, and any Tarnisi who had ever seen active duty on a suppression campaign must well know, that sexual intercourse between the two groups was at such times a matter of simple fact and, indeed, formed no small part of the attractions of the campaign. . . . And surely not all the women who had fled and shrieked had run very fast, for that matter. . . .

For another matter, not every Tarnisi assigned to duty in the Outlands had gone there and lived there with a wife. It was a reasonable assumption that these had not all been celibate. But be the explanations what they may, and certainly they must be many, there did exist a community of part-Tarnisi stock, and by the law of averages at least some members of this community in the course of time would themselves conceive children by Tarnisi parents. Some of these would marry among themselves. Some would drift back into the maternal, native community.

And others . . . others, of course, would attempt to enter the parental, Tarnisi community. And some of them, by that same law of averages, were bound to succeed. Hence in part the hatred and scorn which accompanied the hated name of *Quasi*. And the refusal of the lackland class even to mention the word. —For that matter, the scrupulous care with which Phonorioth had avoided so far mentioning another word.

Feeling his way carefully, Tonorosant said, "Having been

raised in another country, as the Sapient informed you, I did not grow up with the same intense prejudices which so many . . . too many, I think . . . of my people have." His host blinked and blinked and smiled and edged nearer. "I have been interested in the reported activities of a certain tulan and his friends to see that more justice is shown—" here it came, "the Volanth. What do you think about this, my cousin's kin? You will agree, I must hope?"

The old scholar thrust his lower lip out just a trifle and proceeded to look noncommittal and stroke his long, clean white beard. At the mention of the word, Phonorioth had jumped as though scalded; immediately and while Tonorosant was still talking he, Phonorioth, had begun and continued to shake his head violently.

"No!" he exclaimed, as soon as his visitor stopped. "No, no! No, ah! Mistake, the Sir Tonorosant—oh, a great mistake. 'Justice,' it is not a question of justice for the . . . the Volanth. It is only a question of justice for us, for *us!* One cannot compare treatment of civilized with uncivilized peoples. We—we—I ask you, only be fair in your reply—have we not the Seven Signs as well? Do we not also live in houses, read and write, obey the laws, study the classics, paint leaves? Not the others! Not those . . . ah, they are animals, brutes. I could tell you tales of outrages they have committed against us, they would disgust you. It is disgusting just to look upon them! No, no, I assure you, I am against every and any attempt to confuse us with them. It can only harm our legitimate cause. I would act against them with utmost rigor, sir. Drive them back, I say! Drive them back!" He stopped, wiped his face with a trembling hand. And the old man looked at Tonorosant with an expressionless face.

In came the refreshments, and perhaps at just the right time, too. Tonorosant left it to his older guide to make small talk and carry on the conversation. He himself had much to think of. Once again he saw (although his own background had never left him in any doubt) the error of the belief that "suffering purified." Suffering seldom if ever did anything of the sort; suffering seldom if ever convinced a sufferer that suffering in itself was always wrong, because in between this conception and the sufferer almost invariably intervened the immediate and intensely felt conviction that this particular suffering was wrong—that *his* particular suffering was wrong. And, his own suffering over, or at least abated, his whole

93

soul was and remained bent and intent on the end, not that no one should suffer, ever, but that he himself should not suffer, ever. Even if others should suffer.

It might be sad, then, to see how the Quasi Tarnisi, Phonorioth, himself scorned the Volanth. But it was far from surprising. He had spoken with pride of his Pemathi grandfather, his Tarnisi grandmother. He had carefully made no mention of any Volanth forebear, yet he must certainly have had one, however remote. Here, in this community, it was evidently a matter of prestige to be even part Pemathi; the Pemathi had a fairly respected place, after all, and it was certainly higher than that of the Quasi. *But the Volanth had no place!* And it was no wonder, though it was a shame, that their partial descendants hated them. Helots of helots, uncouth, brutal and brutalized, what could they do for their demi-cousins, except remind them of their hated origin?

It was again nothing unexpected that the Quasi, part Tarnisi, part Volanth, should hate—not the Tarnisi who hated them—but the Volanth who by comparison must be guiltless of very great offense. Yes, true, naturally, the Quasi resented the Tarnisi attitude towards themselves, the Quasi. But that was all which they resented in the Tarnisi. Aside from this grievous fault, which they would alter if they could, they held the Tarnisi to be faultless. But who would, who could admire the coarse and outcast Volanth? Tarnisi = Civilization; Volanth = Savagery. True or false, for better or for worse. It was the cultured, smooth Tarnisi whom one imitated, towards whom one aspired. Thus, by iniquitous irony, the styles and standards of the oppressors had become the ideals of even the oppressed. And the relationship from down, looking up, was one of mingled hate-love and love-hate. But from down, looking even farther down, it was nothing but hate.

"—thus," continued Phonorioth, forgetfully wiping at his full mouth with the back of his hand, "we must say: While we will ever appreciate, I must hope, the successful efforts of the Tulan to enable us to register our land titles here in the village, we must absolutely refute his notion that our cause is in any way connected with the beasts of Volanths—"

There was more, but after a while Tonorosant felt he had had enough. It was pathetic, the way the man almost clung to them in hopes of prolonging their stay. They drove on through the shanty-village towards the promise of clean, green quiet in the trees and town ahead. "I had a curious impression as I came into the house," Tonorosant said, "that I saw a rather hideous old woman crouching in front of the mirror for a moment."

"Likely enough," the old man said, placidly.

"It was just for a flash of a second, but it seemed to me that she was plucking hairs from her face!"

"Likely enough."

"Who could it have been?"

"Oh . . . his mother . . . likely enough. . . ."

Jolted into turning his head, Tonorosant looked towards the Sapient, but as his float was not in precise alignment with the other, he actually looked past him. And received an even greater jolt. He looked directly into the open front of a low and dirty drink shop. Amidst the throng of Quasi one seemed to stand out—a man somewhat but not much better dressed than the others, his arm around a loose-bodied woman, he pressing a glass to her lips, she mock-pushing him away. The man didn't look out the front of the groggery, but he moved a bit, urging the glass, and he showed his face —drunken, bitter, yet somehow more relaxed . . . and somehow, very much in place here.

And everything else about him fell very much into place.

"If a Quasi wanted to pass for Tarnisi, it might make sense not to aim too high, mightn't it? and to pose as, say, a lacklander?"

Still placid, "Likely enough," the old sage said again.

The drink shop fell behind. The pleasures of Tarnis Town lay ahead. And behind, too, with all his sullen joys, the man at the dirty bar. Here, at least, Cominthal had no need to pose at all.

CHAPTER EIGHT

The land sloped away and upward as far as the light but incessant rains permitted the eye to see. It was not a country of trees and it was not a cheerful country. The floats had no need of roads or even paths, but something which had worn one deep into the earth. The terrain seemed ancient and weary, the landscape was sullen and wet. Aero-3D shots were being taken all up and down a reticulated area, and from designated spots within each rectangle both core- and surface-samples had to be taken. The somewhat stocky middle-aged man with Tonorosant had long since ceased to be amused.

"Maybe I should have stayed where I was and let *them* reprocess me. At least it would have been dry."

His companion said nothing, continued to set up the drill. Water streamed off both of them and along the ground.

"A tactful silence. But why? I'm sure that you know what I'm talking about."

"Joint, please."

He handed the joint, watched it being fitted into place, shrugged his broad shoulders. "After all, if I weren't the same as you, would I know anything about it?" the stout fellow tried again. No answer. "And if you aren't the same as me, how is it that you don't try to convince me you don't know what I'm talking ab—" The drill spun into action. A burst of mud and air splattered against him. He jumped back and looked on with rueful good humor, shaking his head. The drill did not go very deep or take too long. In a matter of moments he helped slip the core in the container.

At the float Tonorosant said, "Come on. . . . You're getting us all wet." He reached over his still-stumbling helper and adjusted the hood.

"How come you don't say something like, 'You will not wish us to perish by an untimely drowning, I must hope?' See what I mean? You're a simulee . . . or something . . . just like I am. Besides, it already *is* all wet in here. Ah, well. Onward and upward to the next enchanted valley." Beside him, fumbling for the control switch, Tonorosant laughed. "Well, I few! A human being is hidden inside of you after all. Victory," crowed the other man, whose name was Storiogath. "Well, now that the beginnings of communication are observed between us—what in the Hell is this all about?"

Tonorosant shrugged. "Non-military levies are as legal as any other kind. A survey is wanted and a survey is being made."

Storiogath poured a hot drink into two cups, handed one of them to the other "Then you think that the pro-Lords faction is right? *They* claim it's all part of a long-range plan to bring the Volanth under more effective control."

Tonorosant inhaled the spicy steam, sipped. "It could be so," he admitted, after a moment.

His companion gurgled noisily. "Like Hell it could, my sister's armpit. What are the soil samples for, then? The gang that swears by the Guardians, one in particular I have in mind, he *has* to be a genuine native or exile, because he's too stupid ever to have made enough money to—you know—*he* assures me that the Inside Word in his clique is that this is all being done to facilitate assignment of new lands. To those who haven't got any now."

"Mmm," Tonorosant murmured, noncommittally.

Below, the land split apart into a gully, then came together again. Somewhere off in the septentrional distances a patch of light broke through the sky, lengthened, made way for another. A wheel of light turned around above them. Then, one by one, the spokes faded and were gone and all the dimness of the shallow rains returned.

"But I can't swallow that one, either. I don't believe that the Guardians want any new lands to be available. This whole program of theirs is intended to weaken the Lords by creating a demand for the *old* lands that the Lords gave away way back when. I wonder what's behind it all. Don't you?"

Tonorosant glanced at the man. There seemed to be something behind what he had said. But there was so much to wonder about these days. The little box attached to the patrols suddenly began to click and chatter. "Oh, burrs. Time to make another sampling," Storiogath grumbled. "And me still wet from the last one."

Guided by the noise, now loud, now soft, now shrill, now deep, from the little box, they maneuvered the float about. The box gave a little purr of contentment, then fell silent. They put the float down and got out again. The surface sample was a mere dab, a second to take and a second to drop into the container already labeled with the coordinates of the sector; it was setting up the drill which took more time. Tonorosant got a rather low-grade satisfaction from performing the task correctly; Storiogath plainly didn't. He jiggled, grunted, dropped as many things as there were to drop, sucked air through his teeth, groaned, wished he were back in Tarnis Town and that it were sunshine again. But by this time the work of drilling and de-coring had become familiar enough so that Tonorosant was able to do it by himself. He looked up after sliding the top back onto the core container and saw that his supposed helper had wandered away, was standing by himself on a rise of ground, outlined against the pearly mists and soft, slanting rain. Something watchful, wary in his look and stance.

First putting the equipment back into the float, he joined the other, giving him a quizzical look, asking with a gesture to be told what was up. For answer, Storiogath took his notetab out and on it scrawled, *There are people near here somewhere.*

How do you know?—And what if there are?

I can smell and hear, can't I? Who can it be—?

Tonorosant had no answer. Supposedly, this was unpeopled terrain. True . . . there was the trail . . . But it might be an animal trail, or it might be old and disused. Or used only by people going across country from elsewhere to elsewhere. . . . In which case it was possible— He strained his ears, widened his nostrils. At first nothing, then nothing. Still nothing. Then . . . it did seem to him that above and behind the light and continual spatter of the rain he could hear something. Voices? Distant, human voices? It was possible. Possible, too, that in addition to the heavy and by now familiar odor of the wet earth he scented something even heavier but quite different: the raw, sharp odor of human flesh and sweat. Then, too, he thought there might be smoke in the air. And—

Below, quite some ways below, there was a scream. No imagination, this. A scream. And another. And another. And then, out of the rain and the misting far, a woman came running, running, screaming, running—

A naked woman.

Sudden remembrance, fright and fear, rose up and hit him in throat and belly and behind the knees. He jerked, trembled. Behind the running woman, a running man. Behind the naked woman, a naked man.

He gave an outraged, helpless cry. It was not possible for war to have broken out again and reached this ritual stage already. It was not possible for this to be—or was it not?— some not wholly physical, some visual as well as auditory echo, of the events of the last campaign? or any campaign? or all campaigns? a mirage of the angry air and hostile mists, forever re-enacting events so dire as to have implanted their scenes forever on the universal ether?

But this mood lasted only a second. The woman screamed too much. She looked back too much. She screamed too loudly. She ran too slowly. It was impossible not to realize: The woman was not attempting to get away. In Tonorosant's ear came confirming words. "*Some*body's got rancid tastes in games—!" And the woman stumbled, and the woman fell.

But she fell very carefully.

And now it was the man who cried out. Louder even than she. Triumphantly. Obscenely—

They came out of the slanting rain and the long wet shadow, a diagonal line of them, so much alike, so moving-all-at-once their gesture, that it seemed that this, too, might be mirage. Reflection. Multiplication. Arms scooping. Arms flinging back. Arms flinging forward. Stones flying.

Down towards the lying woman the man leaping.

The man flinging up both his arms. The man's legs flying out from under him. The man falling.

But not carefully. And not upon the woman.

And then all the voices crying out. Below, triumph and hatred and scorn. Above, alarm! alarm!

All heads down there upon the lower ground snapped up. This time the woman ran for real, leaping up and skimming over the wet sod, and she ran in the same direction as the running men. She did not scream or cry out even once. And they vanished away as they had come. And the figure lay scattered where they had brought it down. And the rains fell upon it, the rains washed it clean of sweat and of blood, and the rains alone lay lovingly upon it.

* * *

It was frightening, the accuracy with which the stones had hit him. Ankle, knee and jaw had certainly been broken. Spine, probably. Temple and cheekbone crushed. Ribs smashed.

"I'm suspending judgment," Storiogath said, tightly. "And I'm getting the Hell out of here. Oh. Well. . . . Oh, I suppose you're right."

He stripped off his rain mantle, too. One beneath, one above, and thus they began to carry him. It had been a long and difficult way down, and would certainly be a longer and more difficult way up. The same thought occurred to them together.

"Which one of us goes for the float?" Tonorosant put it first.

"Which—? Oh, burrs. Safety in numbers. We'll both go together, my brother's backside, I must hope. Why not? *He* won't be going anywhere without our help."

The rain was cold. "No. . . . But he might go somewhere with someone else's help. And if I've got to bring back a story like this, I'd just as soon bring back the evidence with it. Besides . . .I don't know about those shaggy men. But I think that this one has already paid. Enough. So—"

So Storiogath was deputed to go for the float. Scarcely had he gone from sight when the old man and the old woman appeared. Heads, at first, just heads peering over the side of what one might have taken to be a mere strata-line upon the side of the broken hill but which must evidently have been a shelf with some degree of depth to it. Then the two of them full length, speaking quietly, hands outstretched and empty. Had they intended him harm, they could have already done it. So he showed his own hands, empty and outstretched, and they came down by some way he could not see from where he was.

A trap? As the dead man had, while living, been entrapped? It did not seem likely. Old man and old woman, primal types, archetypes, a nap of snowy hairs like an aureole or halo on bodies and limbs, stooped with age, heedless of the heedless rain, moved—it would seem—by nought but pity for the dead and concern for the living. Plucking at his by now sodden suit and moaning. Gesturing, gesturing. What? Smoke. Ah. Fire. Come with us, dry, warm. This was what they meant. And the dead man?

They assumed that burden themselves. Stooped with age they were, but still strong and agile enough. Tonorosant left his cap and a note, although likely enough he would be able to see the float from above and come out and signal. He followed the old pair and with some effort persuaded the woman to relinquish her hold upon the mantle-covered burden to him; she then went ahead as a guide, frequently turning to point out convenient footholds and putting out her hands to help him.

The ledge was, as he had thought it must be, rather a deep shelving which at its back so undercut the face of the cliff as to constitute a cave. The work of nature had been assisted by crude but sufficient efforts—walls of mud and rock, floor of sand and grass and furry hides. And a fire burned. Of what? there being no trees hereabouts. When he saw the small and smouldering red eye of heat augmented from the neat stack of fuel he thought at first that it must be the dried dung of some animal; but soon enough he realized that it must be peat or something of the sort, cut from a source not too far off with the crude but serviceable tool leaning against the rough wall.

The place had a strong odor all its own, but it was not at all unpleasant—not to one with his rich experience of odors, certainly. The body was set down against the farthest wall. And then as the old woman continued her work at the fire, the old man improvised a sort of rack of smooth, worn poles and indicated to him that he was to put his clothes on them to dry. Just for a moment Tonorosant shivered, but after that, no more. He was just beginning to enjoy the warmth when the old woman moaned.

Tonorosant turned in surprise. The old man gave a cry, too. It was him that they were concerned with—their guest —and, coming up to him, they showed him why.

"Ah, that? It *is* an ugly scar. A bowl of boiling oil turned over—" That was not oil in the pot on the fire, but he mimed the accident by pointing to it: evidently they understood. "It was a long, long time ago. In Pemath. *Pemath.*" They repeated the word, but it did not seem to mean anything to them. Still, they seemed upset and concerned, and they caressed his skin as one might a child's. And for as long as he stayed unclad he saw them glancing back at him and sighing and making a rapid jerking of their heads as though distressed. By and by, whatever was in the pot was prepared and they shared it with him, passing around a battered old spoon of Pemathi make which must have come long ago from some trade packet.

Strange, they seemed not surprised that he would eat with them. Surely no true Tarnisi would put into his mouth anything which had ever been in a Volanth's mouth. But in all probability they had never had occasion to put any true Tarnisi to the touch or test. Even refused commensality likely had not been common enough for them ever to have heard of it. They showed him no hate, no fear, no resentment. Neither did they engage in elaborate shows of how hospitable they were. They were just reacting simply to a simple situation. Neither the dead nor the living were to be exposed to the rain. But the living were subject to wet and cold and hunger and their needs in these respects must be taken care of. That was all.

But was that really all? And was it really that simple? Ah, alas, no. It wasn't at all.

And so, regretfully, but with determination not allowing nasty memory to prevent, he began to mimic. The woman fleeing. The man pursuing. The other men. The thrown stones. The death. And the woman and the other men vanishing. . . . Strange, that he never felt in danger from them! He felt no danger at all here. But it was clear that the old man and woman understood. Of their explanation, if that was what it was, he understood nothing. Their gestures conveyed nothing, neither did the excited gutturals and plosives which burst upon the air . . . nothing, that is, but regret and dismay. Which made it even stranger yet: that *they* were not afraid of *him*. Which, after all, considering, they had every right to be.

From below a noise, a sound, tossed by the winds, muffled by the rains. He darted from the cave and from the ledge he could see his companion of the survey. On foot, with no sign of the float. Tonorosant cupped his hands around his mouth and shouted. And again. Until Storiogath saw him at last. The old man was already on his way down and Tonorosant obeyed the old woman's gestures and returned to shelter. By the time the others had returned, his clothes had dried.

"Where's the float?" he asked his panting friend.

A gasp, a gesture and look of complete bewilderment—"It's not there! It's not there—!"

They demonstrated this as best they could to the old one, who grasped it in a moment. He and his wife broke into excited talk. In a few moments it seemed arranged that they were to follow the old man. He knew where it was?—Where it might be? He knew, at any rate, *some*thing.

"All right, then, we'll go with him," said Storiogath. He was unhappy, wet. He gestured to the still form at the back of the cave. "But we need the rain suits more than he does now." Tonorosant agreed.

It grew perceptibly darker as they followed the aged guide along a trail visible only to him. He was long silent. When he spoke it was with a wordless groan. Evidently he had hoped to find something which was no longer there. What it was he soon showed them. In the sodden grass he paced an outline, gestured to them to see how it was pressed down within the area . . . an area the size of a float. And, just where the vents would be, he showed them the grass shriveled as though by a jet of steam. It was still faintly warm to the touch.

"This does us up good. My mother's mammary! Who stole our float?" Storiogath pressed his hands to his head. "Not that it matters . . . or why he put it down here. It couldn't have been a Volanth—"

"Obviously. But what just struck me isn't as obvious. This wasn't our float."

"Wasn't— What do you mean?"

"Look at the outline. Too small. It was a different model— one of the older ones."

The other studied the rain-swept ground a moment before nodding. "You're right. A Y-rack. So—"

Slowly, guessing out loud—"There were two of them. The one back in the cave was the other. They came and put down here. Well. Then there were the fun and games, but only that one participated. The other one went . . . somewhere else . . . maybe to watch . . . maybe to do something else. Anyway— He saw us. And while we were down below or on our way down, he took our float. Made it back here quickly. And then took off quickly. So— If I'm right—"

He started out in a widening spiral. Almost at once the old man understood what he intended. The three of them tracked outward from the place where the other float had been. And by and by they found what they were looking for: their own float, wedged into a gulley.

"It shouldn't be too hard to wiggle her out of there."

"It wouldn't be if he hadn't taken the starting-cam with him."

It could have been worse, much worse. The craft might have been wrecked, defueled, blown up, damaged in a variety of ways, Tonorosant thought. This way they at least had food and shelter until their signals might bring relief. Whoever it was had done it had shown them fair courtesy. It was all very odd.

When he turned to see the old man, though, he saw only that he had gone. The two of them sat inside and talked and watched it darken and watched it rain while they waited.

* * *

His up-seat comfortably adjusted so that he could both see the ceiling screen and reach for his drink, Tonorosant lay back and regarded the reflected paragraph for the tenth or twentieth time.

The increasing chemo-industrial utility of oron-oil has begun to show signs of overtaking its utility as a product intended mainly for consumption as food. In the past five years, oron-oil to the value of ten million units has been converted into synthetics, and the process shows no signs of slackening. This new use for an old produce comes barely a generation after the former haphazard methods of cultivation in the Isles of Ran

His thumb pressed the tiny control box resting on his chest and half of the text slid up and away and was replaced on the ceiling screen by more. But it was no use. He was still not able to concentrate, still—between his mind and the text— the events of the previous day persisted in intervening. Once again he saw the chase, the false chase ending in death. There within his opulent room so safe from the discomforts of nature a slanting rain continued to fall. He smelled, not the scented wood of his own walls, but the reek of the turf fire in the cave.

It was Hob Sarlamat who had set down next to them in the distant darkness, Sarlamat in a double-motor float large enough for all of them.

"Didn't you bring a replacement?" Tonorosant asked, motioning to the empty place where the starting-cam had been.

He shook his head. "I left before we got your signal. In fact, I left as soon as that," he indicated the little box whose purpose was to guide them in making their landings at the proper places to test and drill, "as soon as that started sending erratically, and I realized that something was wrong."

"So you're in on this, too?—This scrape-and-drill levy, I mean."

Sarlamat's thin face twisted impatiently. "Do you think we can leave it all up to the sons of the Seven Signs? They'd get bored to death and drop it by the third day. . . . What happened?"

He listened, frowning, rubbing his eyes. At last he said, "At least let's transfer the soil samples." And that, for a while, was that. Later, in answer to questions about the body, he said that "it would have to keep till morning." He would voice no notion as to what it all meant or could mean, but—"I think the two of you have earned a release from levy-duty for the present," he said, as lights began to show with increasing frequency. "I'll see to it."

"'Earned' it? I should think we have, my father-in-law's fanny, I must hope to Hell we've earned it—"

But Sarlamat wasn't finished. "One condition, though—Keep this quiet. All of this. Agreed?"

Tonorosant said he had a condition of his own. "Will you— Can you see to it, too, that the old Volanth and his wife aren't bothered?—when the body is picked up? Or afterwards?"

His friend's eyelids had dropped a bit and his mouth had set a bit, as though he had not cared for anyone else's making conditions. But when he heard what the conditions were, a spasm of annoyance had passed over his face. "Of course, of course. Need you have bothered?"

Perhaps not, Tonorosant now thought. Nothing in the actions of Sarlamat and his associates had indicated that they would be likely to find pleasure in Tarnisi-style violence. He tried once again to concentrate on his book. If he hoped some day to be a planter and an island owner, it behooved him to begin to learn something more of the economics of the whole scene than the little he knew now.

> *This new use for an old product comes barely a generation after the former haphazard methods of cultivation on the Isles of Ran gave way to the current techniques of industrial agriculture. The old-style "planter" seldom if ever actually planted anything, contenting himself with the gathering of the oron-nuts as they happened to ripen and fall. In terms of labor force and production schedules this was hopelessly inefficient, producing less than the value of one million units in an average year. The introduction of efficiency-oriented plantations had to wait upon the establishment of efficiently planted groves. The first of these was the Model Experimental Station in North Oto-Ran which began its operations in the year 0756 under the sponsorship of the gigantic Commerce-Lermencas combine. The scattered clusters. . . .*

He yawned, blinked, stretched. Wished that Atoral was there with him. The wish was not even erotic. He would like just to be next to her and to fall asleep in her arms. But she had finally whisked her sister away from the stuffy atmosphere of idealistic confusion in the old tulan's home and was now occupied with setting the girl up in a town cottage of her own. Resolutely, he turned back to his book, jiggled the control. A moment later he was sitting bolt upright, swearing, pounding his fist upon his thigh.

He found Storiogath in the company of a rumpled and sullen-eyed lackland girl who left without a word even while he was apologizing for his hasty and unexpected entry. Stori cut short the further apologies prompted by this.

"Never mind, and in fact—just as well. Those double-L females are all the same, anyway. Very unsubtle. First they climb all over you and then afterwards they insist that you marry them. Marry! If I'd wanted to *marry* I could have stayed where I was, my nephew's neurons, I must hope—so what is it brings you here all of a flurry? A *book?* What— feelthy pictures? No. So—*Insular Industrial Arboriculture*— now, what in the Hell?"

He subsided and watched as his companion of the previous day fitted the book-cartridge into the projector, dutifully reading each sentence as it proceeded up the screen towards oblivion. " 'Commerce-Lermencas,' " he said. "They don't come much bigger, do they? But what—"

"Be quiet and read on."

Stori obediently closed his mouth, raised his eyebrows.

The scattered clusters of oron-trees were all removed and the land left free for replanting in planned, co-ordinated groves. In order that this might be done with maximum efficiency and the resultant trees be identical in size, the following system was used. Aero-3D shots were taken all up and down a reticulated area, and from designated spots within each rectangle both core- and surface-samples were taken. By this method the necessity of working with and not against the terrain, plus the equally important matter of plus-, minor-, and mean-factors in the surface and sub-surface soil . . .

In a stifled voice, Stori said, "My brother-in-law's balls—"

"You wondered if either the Lords or the Guardians were behind the Survey," Tonorosant reminded him. "And, to tell you the truth, I was puzzled about that, too. Well, now we know. It's neither. And we not only know who *isn't*.

"We know who *is*."

CHAPTER NINE

The rest of the page lacked the shock value of that one paragraph, but it was nonetheless informative.

Stori said, "But that wasn't oron-tree country."

"No, it isn't. That's beside the point. Which is, that that country—and I suppose, sooner or later, most of Tarnis—is being readied for factory-type agriculture. There are other crops beside oron-nut oil. We know who is behind the survey. The Craftsmen. And we also know—now—who is behind the Craftsmen."

"Commerce-Lermencas. Which means Lermencas itself . . ." Stori mused. "Which means . . . all kinds of things. Who's going to supply that 'well-regulated labor force' the book talks about, do you suppose?"

"Oh, Commerce-L. is going to supply the regulation, you may be sure of that. As for the labor, well, I guess that's where the Volanth come in."

"Pshwew. . . . The poor hairy lack-lucks. No more piddling along at their own pace, with now and then a pleasant pause to play the he and she game. Too bad. Too bad."

But Tonorosant didn't think it was too bad at all. He wasn't at all sure but what the bad might be outweighed by the good. Stori was hardly taking a realistic view of the scene. There was nothing Arcadianly picturesque in the life the Volanth led. They toiled to set up fish-weirs . . . along came a boat and knocked them down, just for fun. They slaved to make their crops, gather resin, cut and fashion timber . . . along came a little war which was still big enough to steal most of their surplus and spread murder and rape. This was the way things had been and as long as the Tarnisi stayed on top, it seemed, this was the way things would always be.

"And you think that the Craftsmen have been setting this up all along, this whole program of changing peoples' bodies and giving them additional minds, planting them here and there where we can be of the most use to them, mixing in local politics—all of this, to help the Volanth?" Stori's whole stocky body expressed his complete scepticism.

Tonorosant gave a one-sided smile. "Of course not. The Craftsmen, which is to say the Lermencasi, it seems, are completely selfish. But their selfishness is a modern one, it doesn't reek of blood and cruelty like the selfishness of the Tarnisi. The Volanth could hardly be worse off, working for wages on huge, supervised management-farms, than they are now. Keep romance out of this. It doesn't belong here, it's a lie. The truth is inescapable: the Volanth would be much better off. Furthermore, they won't remain just laborers forever. The Lermencasi are practical. They'll set up schools. Once you start that process, there's no way to stop it. First, some Volanth will be trained to perform minor tasks. And, gradually, by the usual sort of reverse gravity, others will begin drifting upwards. Lermencas is part of the modern world; Tarnis isn't. The Volanth aren't. But they are going to become part of it, from now on. And eventually, either with Lermencasi help or without it, the Volanth are going to have what they ought to have: a share in running their own country."

Stori nodded, mused a moment. Shrugged. "Well, I don't begrudge it to them, my aunt's navel, I must hope. If the Craftsmen want to give me a job running a sanitary nut-farm and teaching the Volanth not to blow their noses with their fingers, it's fine with me. There's just one or two minor details, though. Agreed, out in Volanth country, the Tarnisi are rogues. But most of the time they're not there, they're here. And here they're rather pleasant people. Charming, gracious. If we didn't all think so, we wouldn't have come here. The obvious question is: What's going to become of the Tarnisi? Aren't they entitled to have a share in running their own country, too?"

Tonorosant grimaced, began walking up and down the room, pulling his fingers. After a while he said, almost grudgingly, "That's the big bump in the road. Ideally, the job of moving into the real world is one they ought to be doing themselves. But they are never going to do it. They can submit to being dragged along into it—or they can resist. Either way, they won't like it. Naturally. I suppose that no one thing is going to happen to all of them. Some, I suppose, will be pensioned off to just flit around being decorative: the Lermencasi are bound to develop the tourist industry; as of now it doesn't exist. Some—damned few, I suppose—

will manage to adjust and fit into the action. More of them in the next generation, inevitably.

"But . . . as for the others . . . the ones who'd have a fit if anyone who lacks the Seven Signs outclassed them . . . the ones who can't even lead a normal sex life without regular bouts of an abnormal sex life at the expense of others—those will go under. They must go under. I don't see that there's any other way.

"No, no. I just don't see that there's any other way."

* * *

And in the darkness Atoral moved closer and put her arm around him. He kissed her shoulder. She said, into his ear, "Is everyone upset these days? My sister was bound to become upset and my father has always been upset. But you, Tonoro? There was a time when you, at least, were not upset. What is this disturbing spirit which is in you?"

"How do you know that I'm upset?"

"*How do I know?* Ah, Tonoro! Oh—it's not as bad as it was after you returned from levy, and that it never will be, I must hope. . . . But you sigh all night and you turn all night and you seldom smile. And I know that it is not me."

"Ah, no! And it will never be you, I must hope!"

He returned her impulsive embrace, then her caress of a moment earlier. His lips found hers in the darkness. Their lips moved, but their hands moved more. And then their bodies. Later, "she listened through his skin to his slowing heart," as an ancient poet had written. Marvelously, for the moment, at peace, he soon slipped away into sleep. He. But not she.

Such peace, however, does not last forever, and while it may diminish other troubles, it cannot abolish them.

It was their custom that, when they were together, they never were always together. "Thus we shall avoid being bored with one another, I must hope," she'd said. Now in the morning she had her self-appointed task—planting several slips and saplings which she had brought from her golden garden; it was her intention to create one for him in a tiny corner of his own garden to remind him of her when she was not there. So her own morning was to be taken up with something she wanted to do and the doing of which would make her happy. But for him—? There was nothing, he found, that he then desired doing. The thought of happiness seemed very far away.

At first he had been happy here in Tarnis merely realizing aspects of his dreams about the land and people. Before this and besides this and even after this, there were his hopes and plans for the future to which Tarnis was nothing more than a gorgeous stepping-stone. The dream had become a familiar reality and it had not been enough, and that hoped-for future he had seen as worthless because selfish: a landscape with only one figure, and more: the gorgeous stepping-stone was stained in blood. So he had pledged himself to wash it clean. Which meant doing as the Craftsmen bid. One might have thought his bitter years in Pemath would have made him suspicious enough forever, so that he would trust no man's motives. And yet, somehow, in this case, it had not. He had made no effort to look behind the Craftsmen . . . despite the words of Mothiosant. *There are some debts which are never paid.* Well, now he had looked. And he had found, oh, not a demon, nor anything as picturesque as that; he had found behind them the hugeness of the cluster of huge corporations known collectively as Commerce-Lermencas. It did not now much surprise him. Even if the physical and psychical surgery and all the cloak and scalpel work of the Craftsmen by now could pay for itself, it would have taken something the size of Commerce-L. or the government of great Lermencas itself to have set it up in the first place.

But all of that made no matter now. He was more than resigned to what the Lermencasi intended; he favored their intention. If the aristocracy of Tarnis must fall, then let it fall. It would fall without much blood—perhaps without any blood at all. But the prospect of the moderate and efficient Lermencasi rule could not inspire with enthusiasm. His mood now alternated between a nervous agitation which had no visible cause and a listlessness which had no visible cure. Thus he paced about his grounds or sank down upon the grass and stared at the water. A time before, beset with heaviness of heart, he had tried to swim his troubles away, naked flesh in naked water, often so chill and cold in the misty morning that it burned like fire. *You like to swim. . . . Yes. . . .* The words now rolled slowly through his mind, and bore associations of bafflement and unpleasantness. Who had said it? What was the occasion?

You swim much. . . .

Cominthal had said it.

The occasion was Tonorosant's entertainment for those somehow connected with the pro-Guardian faction—but that hardly mattered. Tonorosant had indeed swum much. But he had never observed anyone observing him. His eyes roved around the water, took in the immaculate grass and the slender, newly planted trees. No . . . not there. But there, *there* across the water, were three or four old trees which had grown wide as they had grown tall. Someone might easily have observed him from there . . . without being observed.

The only question was, *Why?*

The wry thought occurred to him, as he made his way through the shacks and shanties of Greenrivers village and dodged with remembering feet the rubble and ordure, that this might well be the first time in history that anyone had ever tried to pass for Quasi! Since no precedents existed and he had no one else's experience to guide him, he was utterly on his own. On him was his by no means best suit of clothes, and he was (standing back from himself and even admiring his own—he hoped—virtuosity in the role) trying his very best to look like someone who often tried to look both Tarnisi and invisible but who was now under no immediate necessity of looking either . . . yet unable to stop, completely.

He paused before each open-fronted drink shop to look in. So far, none of them seemed to be the right one, but at least no one seemed to find his curiosity objectionable, or even peculiar. Now and then a counterman, seeing him, would call out, encouragingly, "Drinkies! Girlies! Eats!"— and return to other tasks with a shrug when he passed on without entering. Often enough a woman, who might be wrinkled or ordinary or comely or barely nubile, would extend a hand or a glass towards him in invitation. Or call out, "Hey, Tulan! Bed?"

But the one who caught his attention at last neither looked up nor said anything. It was not the same place, but it seemed to be the same woman. She had on last night's makeup and last week's dress and she was no longer pretending to refuse a proffered drink. In fact, she was begging one from the counterman. *Try*ing to beg one. Tonorosant put money on the counter and slanted his head. At first her attention was all on the glass and getting it down and she gave him no more than a glance from the corner of her bleared eyes. Her features were strongly Volanth and it was strange to realize that she might have spent her childhood in some distant hut or cave . . . and all which that implied . . . before being swept up by a current she probably little understood, to be deposited here, upon the dungheap of a culture which had both begotten and disowned her.

Over the second drink, which she took more slowly, she gave him a direct look and tried to smile out of her smeared mouth. The effort and its effect gave him a pang of pain. "What you looking fow, Tulan? Fun? You buy me thwee dwinks, I give you fun, cheap. . . ." Her look grew both impressed and puzzled. "What bwing you he'e?—because you, you cou' pass, so easy. . . ." But the strain of wondering was too hard, and she dissolved it in her drink. The third one found her both cheerful and informative. Cominthal? Yes, she did know him. A sport, a spender, and a real tulan. Where he was *now?* Well . . . that depended.

It depended only on another drink for her and a small coin for a small boy, who led him through alleys and wastes and, it had begun to seem, might have led him on forever, if a man had not stepped out of a house somewhat sturdier than the average and said, simply, "Over here."

There was some sort of a shop up front but in a moment a door or a screen shut out sight and sound of it. A small lamp under a tattered shade supplied all the light there was. It was stuffy and contained more smells than one would have thought possible. An old woman remarkably ugly squatted on the floor and plucked at her lips. Cominthal, looking no more sullen, no more bitter than usual, said, "I know what you're looking for."

"Oh . . ." It was in his mouth to say that he scarcely knew himself, but all he did say was, "What?"

Cominthal reached into a curtained recess, grunted, came out with a something wrapped and tied, fumbled with it. And again Tonorosant said, "Oh . . ." There, in the other's hand, was the starter-cam of a float.

The other man's look slid from his. "I didn't hurt you," he said. "I didn't even hurt your float . . . just slowed you up."

Tonoro had been right. Two men, besides himself and Stori, had come upon that melancholy scene. And one hadn't left it alive. "Who was the dead man?" he asked.

A shrug. "Some Lord's brother, some Guardian's son, I suppose. I don't care. I pimp, you know," he said, looking into a corner and almost indifferent in his tone. "There's nothing else for me to do. Not yet. He wanted that and he paid me to fix it up. I hired the woman. Didn't hire the men. That happens, sometimes, you know." He looked up now and now looked Tonoro not merely eye to eye but it seemed pupil to pupil. "You should know," he said. Not indifferently.

"I?—I don't know why I should. And I didn't come about that, anyway."

The old woman ceased pulling her lips and looked at the newcomer with a sort of loving leer. "So pwetty," she said. "So smooth, oh so smooth. But sometimes it gwows haiwy as it gwows older. . . ."

"She's brockety," Cominthal said. "She's been brockety for forty years." He laid his finger against his head. "You don't know. So. Not anything? Not a single thing?" His voice grew more interested, but did not grow more warm.

Tonoro said nothing for a moment. Then he asked, "You hid and watched me swimming. Why?"

"I didn't know why at first. Then I thought: Something about him I must find out. What? The way he carries his head? Why?—So I hid. And I watched. But you don't know. So—" He said something in his throat and chest rather than his mouth. Something sounding like, " '*Kh ghoroum- 'akhagh*—"

There was a grunt and a shuffle. The red-figured curtain hanging before the recess was parted by what Tonoro first thought was a bundle of twigs. Behind it came a head and behind the head a body—so small, so light, it seemed scarcely human. This was not only the oldest old Volanth which he'd ever seen, it was past a doubt the oldest human being he had ever seen. He crawled forward on his twiggy fingers and hands and on his shriveled knees, and all the while his filmy eyes took in Tonoro's appearance. His voice was, incredibly, still deep, but its echoes were curious rather than impressive. Tonoro said, "Who—?" and stopped.

"*Gorum*. He makes gorum." Then, impatiently, as one explains the obvious to the willfully ignorant: "He is the *gorum* man." Faint flickerings of recollection in Tonoro's mind. A Volanth word, one of the very, very few known to the Tarnisi despite close to a thousand and half a thousand years of proximate contact—and perhaps only because of its being mentioned in the national epic, *The Volanthani*. So—*gorum*. Religion? Medicine? Magic? Witchcraft? Hypersensual perception? Thaumaturgy? None of these, perhaps, or not quite any of these, or perhaps something a little different from all of these. But—He *makes* gorum? How are such things made?

The eyes were not so filmy, after all. A strange golden-brown, the eyes. *"Ghoroum—'akhaghi thghasht,"* the ancient voice said, rumbling and echoing. It repeated the words, or perhaps it said other words, the sound become odder and odder as it sank deeper and deeper. Tonoro listened, astonished at first, then incredulous: the old, old, very old man was no longer speaking in his throat, or even in his chest. Quite certainly the words were now coming from his withered and sunken old belly; one could see the skin and the flaccid muscles moving! And then, aghast, Tonoro heard the sound still sounding in the paunch but heard it now grow higher, higher, thinner, shriller, younger. His mouth opened upon a soundless note of infinite amazement. The muscles of his own stomach crawled to realize the voice now within it, voice now ascending to his own chest, his own throat, piping, piping, tuneless song.

Song which went on and on and on as all time ceased forever and all sight and all.

* * *

The young bloods, the levy-men, had circled the village round about, but the village did not realize it yet. It was early, quite early in the morning, gray and filmy as such times usually were, with mists curling up from the small rivers. Here and there a baby cried, was quickly taken to the breast, cried no more. An old man coughed himself awake, gurgled into silence . . . silence broken only by the old woman's cracking twigs for the fire. By and by there would be something—not much—hot to drink; with luck, before the old man began to cough again. A younger woman sighed and stretched on her pallet and began to get up and set about things, was prevented by an arm from across the pallet. For a moment she resisted, then sighed again, lay back. For the while, at least, morning would wait outside. Two young boys awoke, scratched, looked at each other, and were still a moment. Then they got up and went outside and piddled.

This small pleasure was soon over and then came the question of what to do next. Even the younger was far too big to be suckled, and the other was twice his size. That there was nothing to eat in the box both knew, for each had arisen stealthily by himself in the night and gone and felt. So they fell to grubbing with their toes in a pile of mussel shells.

The bigger one tired of this first. "They're going to get you," he said; watched to see the result.

"No. No, they're not...." The small one lacked conviction. "Why?" he asked.

"Because you haven't got a license."

But in giving a reason he had given away his cause. The small one had ears, too. "*You* haven't got a . . . a . . ." His tongue faltered over the word.

"I don't need one. I can pass. You do. You can't. You have hair." His filthy finger riffled the down on the small one's skinny arm, pimpling the skin as it passed.

"So do you. You have—"

But the bigger one grabbed for him, face scowling. "Don't you say that!" The other hesitated. He could break and run. Or he could aim a kick at the testicles before running. Or he could just stay and take the coming blow. If he escaped it now he would only catch it later. He hunched up his shoulders, prepared to yell. Inside the shack the noises had stopped, which the boys had heard with no more reflection than if they had been snores. The woman sighed once more. The man made a satisfied noise in his chest. Then he was there, looming up above them, cocking his head, a slight smile.

"Cousins, don't fight," he said. "Don't fight."

"Uncle, I want something to eat," the bigger boy said immediately. The small boy said nothing, but took the man's hand. He knew the man was his father, knew the woman inside was not his mother. He knew no memory of a mother. He knew that if the man found something to eat that all would eat. He also knew that there was no food in the shack, but the look on his father's face told him that the man knew where food was and had both hope and intention of finding it.

"Now," the man began a sentence which was never finished. His mouth went round, his face went stiff, his hand clenched upon the hand of the child. From one side came a continuous series of sounds of a sort which the boy had never heard before—a sort of rushing noise, ending in a flat, dry clap. Again and again. In the middle of this a woman began to scream, high and shrill. A man's voice called out something in a note of ever-rising urgency which in a moment became a baying of sheer pain. In another second this was drowned out by voices shouting—harsh and hysterical and violent. One second's silence followed and then from all sides, like the growing hum of a swarm of insects, the village questioned from within what it had just heard from without. And then found its answer. And all the noise and all the sound became one as the people poured into the streets and the raiders poured into the village.

All the while father and son, in that swift series of seconds which were all the while, held their hands conjoined. Then the man's grip loosened, the boy's clasp tightened. His father bent down and said—said—did not scream, "Now you have to go and hide in that hole I showed you. You remember where it is? You go and hide there until I tell you to come out, or until it gets dark. Go, now. Run. Run."

And because his father had spoken without urgency, so the boy began to run without urgency. He knew very well where the hole was and liked the game of hiding there. It did not occur to him at the first that he had to be afraid. Few things, though, are more contagious than fear, and of these the first is panic. And in no more than a moment the streets, the alleys, lanes and all the other open spaces were filled with people running blindly, running madly, running into each other and upon each other and over each other, and the people were filled with panic.

Behind them, before them, pouring in from all sides were the raiders of the levy. They had things in their hands and from these came the constant noise of *whoosh-whoosh—smack!* and with each *smack* a house or hovel began to smoulder and then burst into flame. In a matter of seconds only the boy saw a woman fall, screaming, beating at her clothes with frenzied hands. Then another. Then another. The populace became a mob. It ran in circles, it leaped into the air, it fell and crawled upon the ground. Nothing stopped, not the noise, not the fire, not the attack. Float after float crashed and smashed the fleeing people. The houses burned, the people burned, the very ground burned, and only blood flowed and it could not put the fire out.

The boy ran, the boy jumped, the boy crawled, rose, ran, fell, rose and hopped and ran again.

Along the edge of one of the streets was a row of ramshackle stalls from which food was hawked, and one merchant had gotten up early to prepare the fritters of plain dough which was all that most of the people would have for breakfast—if they were lucky enough to have any breakfast. He had fled with the first wave and wherever he was now he must already have learned that there was nowhere to flee, his flour and batter lay unattended and unbothered, his fire still burned and his pot of oil still boiled. The naked boy no longer knew where his hideyhole was but he still ran because he knew of nothing else to do, he was still running when the mob stampeded into the row of stalls, knocking their flimsy structures flat, he was still running when the hot oil splashed upon his naked flesh and seared it and made him open his mouth in breathless pain. He ran on and he screamed and he ran and he ran. The air was hot and still and the noises were hideous, frightening, unfamiliar; he was running, running, running, they were behind him and beside him and then they were ahead of him and his head hurt his side hurt his feet hurt, he dared not stumble, he turned aside, he no longer saw, and he ran and he ran and he *ran*—

* * *

The old man was still piping and muttering, but within Tonoro was the even physical memory that the voice had just departed from his own body. He looked into the *gorum*-man's golden-glowing eyes. Already they seemed to be filming over. The voice became a thin trickle of sound and then it, too, was only memory.

Cominthal looked at him with an expression that was half leer and half triumph. "So now you know," he said. "Now you remember and you know."

"Yes . . . now I know. . . ."

"You are a Quasi. Just the same as me and the brockety old woman and all the rest of us. You're part Volanth, you know that? You know it?" The word he said was *know* but the word he meant was *admit*.

Some faint disappointment showed in his face. Perhaps he had expected Tonoro to cringe, curse, shrink, cower. . . . Perhaps if the implanted memories were the only ones, Tonoro might have done so. Some shock on this point the newly awakened was aware of, but there were so many other things to engage him—part Volanth. Well, and then, part-Tarnisi, too! He remembered the words of the Craftsman in Pemath, *"Fortunately, you already have long fingers and slender feet."* Fortunately—but not fortuitously: the gift of his Tarnisi genes.

"I know it now. But—how did *you* know it?"

The look was all triumph now. "At first it was just that

something about you kept catching my attention. I didn't know what. After a while it came to me that the way you sometimes carried your head, that was it, it was reminding me of the way the uncle used to carry *his* head. So I kept looking and I kept watching. Nothing else about you that I could *see* . . . but you had come back, they said, from abroad. Well, they have big *gorum* abroad, too. With that foreign *gorum* it would be easy to make big changes. Then, after that I spoke to you on the levy, after we came back from that—oh, that was a thing, eh? how did you like that? How do you like it *now*? Now that you *know*? Ah;—then I used to hide and I watched you and watched you when you went swimming."

"And you saw the scar?"

"I saw the scar. So then I knew for sure. And now *you* know for sure."

Cominthal his cousin! Something of the boy still remained in the man, now that he, Tonoro, could remember. Something cruel and stunted and yet eager and avid and hungry. There was so much to remember, and so much that—

Gorum! Yes, it could be said that there was "big *gorum*" abroad, but the supposedly savage, supposedly primitive and brutal and debased (and all the rotten rest of it) Volanth need not shame to compare their own skills with those of any others. Not even with the Craftsmen. . . . So much to remember. It was making him feel sick and anguished and confused. He didn't want to talk about it all now, or even part of it. He only wanted to lie down and rest. Rest.

It surprised him that Cominthal understood and was willing. Afterwards, they talked much together.

The raid, that raid of the levy-men upon the village so long ago, had not even the justification of the recent one in which both Tonoro and Cominthal had taken part. No accusation of murder existed; it had been enough that most of the Quasi villagers, being technically Volanth, had required licenses to live outside the Outlands—outside Volanth country—and most of them had lacked them. This was sufficient excuse. This, and the ever-existent unhealthy urges of the Tarnisi to break loose of their over-sophisticated and boring way of life—break loose, break out, burn and slay and ravish: the beast inside, ravening, always, against mannered restraint, had gotten outside. And had had its way.

Afterwards, the levy-men glutted (for the present while), and boasting of their prowess and of the "lesson" taught, had gone away. Slowly, slowly, the survivors had picked themselves up and, dazed, but as always, acquiescent, begun the job of burying their dead and tending to their wounded. Rebuilding their homes. Rebuilding their lives. Tonoro (he had of course been called something else then, but it hardly seemed important, now, exactly what) had somehow dragged himself at last to the appointed hideyhole, after it was no longer necessary; and there he had been found at last by his father—scalded, burned, anguished, racked by pain and thirst, but withal obedient and faithful.

"He saw that it couldn't go on," said Cominthal.

It couldn't—but it always had. Would it always? The man said, *No*. The boy's burn was a long time in healing, a healing which had made that familiar scar, left by the Craftsmen to whom it meant nothing, recognized at last by Cominthal. And all the while it was healing the man had gone from friend to friend, from friend's friend to friend's friend, mostly at night and always behind closed doors and shut screens, in voice low and stealthy, and had spoken the incredible, impossible, heart-stirring words: *It must not go on forever*. It need not go on. It will be stopped.

It must!

Small coin was added to small coin, tiny hoard to tiny hoard. The harlots' hire and the profits of pimps. The sweat of those who toiled at the tasks even the Pemathi desired not to do and hired others to do for them. The takings of thieves and the meager profits of shanty traders. A compact was made and a league was formed, oaths taken. Promises. Plans. Hopes that almost did not dare to exist. But only "almost."

"We bribed Pemathi," Cominthal recalled (forgetting that at his then age he could hardly have been counted among the *we*), "and got you both aboard a cargo ship. He wouldn't go without you," Cominthal said, mouth twisting in remembered envy. "The both of you going off for freedom, and me staying behind to lie in the dust and the dung—" It was long before he could be gotten to believe that his younger cousin, too, had lain long in the dust and the dung. "I don't even remember where the ship was bound for. It hardly mattered. He was to make contact with foreigners. *Any* foreigners. To promise them anything, anything at all, just to get them to help. To help us here. Against *them*. The ones with the Seven Signs." He ran his tongue out a little ways upon his lips. "To strip every one of those Signs from them. . . ." His voice descended into whispered obscenities.

"But what happened?" asked Tonoro.

"Ah? What do you mean?—'Happened?' "

"With my father."

Cominthal stared at him. "You still don't know? Don't remember? Even now?"

Even now. The *gorum* had not restored every lost memory, it became quite clear. It had indeed restored the one dreadful one which the mind had almost succeeded in its attempt to forget. But the boy had been young, then, so very young . . . and the other memories, which would have, probably, been lost anyway—these stayed lost. "I suppose," he said now, slowly, "that the cargo ship must have put into Pemath. It wasn't a good place for a beginning. Anything could have happened to him. He could have been killed for a piece of bread. I wish I knew," he said, then crying the words: "*I wish I knew!*" To have the memory of a father restored at last, precious gift. Then to find the memory so incomplete, tragic loss. Loss, loss, loss, never to be regained. Some things are lost forever, and, seemingly, this was one of them.

Some things are lost forever.

But Cominthal would not suffer him—and this was good, that he would not—to remain there, wandering and disconsolate in the broken shatters of the past; in Pemath, with all its bitter and its inconclusive memories. Memories which had been so confused . . . it was not in Pemath, then, that the scald-scar was formed. And not in Pemath that the memories of pursuit were made. It meant nothing to any other victims of the infamous child-hunts of the evil Old Port that this one boy had never been one of them. It meant, somehow, though, much to him.

But Cominthal said, "You see, don't you. . . . You saw! It's still going on! And it must not go on. They still treat us like the Volanth treat fish: snare them, kill them, gut them, eat them. Even though what's theirs by right of blood is ours by right of the same blood. We have to stop it. Don't we? All of us? Even you. You know that now.

"Even you."

Tonoro looked around the crowded, musty mockery of a room. The old man had crawled back into his recess. The mad old woman had gone away somewhere, perhaps to examine for the millionth time her hopelessly ugly, hopelessly hairy face in the mirror. Outside swarmed the jetsam outcasts of the civilized and heedless aristocracy. Across from him sat the cousin of his own blood: by his own testimony, a pander. It was a curious homecoming. Could all these ever be the features of true home? He could scarcely conceive so.

"Yes," he said.

"Even me."

CHAPTER TEN

Night in the garden at Tonoro's riverside house lacked, no doubt, the sophisticated charm of the justly famed night gardens of many older estates. Although most of the flowers and trees were diurnals, and no attempts had been made to encourage or maintain nocturnal songbirds, still, walking among his greenery even when it was too dark to appreciate it by sight—save for that revealed by the rare and semi-concealed lamps—had always been a pleasure to him. It was the hour of the first dew. He was alone.

He had much to consider. Confusion had been lessened only a little in one direction, that of his own background, and he had lived with its lapses for so long that they'd ceased to trouble him; confusion in every other direction had only been increased. He was, it now seemed, doubly yoked, for not only was he bound to the Craftsmen and their cause, he was bound to the Quasi and their cause, too. How did the two fit together? Or did they fit together at all? What was the main thing to be achieved? He had to decide on this, and then see if it afforded or could afford a common denominator.

The liberation of the Volanth and the Quasi from the cruelty and terror and stultifying conditions imposed upon them by the Tarnisi: surely this was the point of it all. The back of the aristocratic system had to be broken, the humane elements among the Tarnisi allowed to come forward without fear—Tulan Tarolioth and his supporters—and the work of introducing all three elements of the population into the main stream of human culture and progress had to be begun.

Something of this had passed between the two men there

in the ramshackle house where the *gorum*-man hibernated behind his curtain.

"The chance may come very soon," Tonoro said, cautiously.

"Not 'may.' *Will*."

"You . . . know about it, then? Do we speak of the same thing?"

And Cominthal's curious comment was, "That remains to be seen. It's sure that you can help us—you've lived abroad. And that's the place our help will come from—abroad."

This fit, certainly. But did he, Tonoro, fit? Really fit? Was the tie of blood sufficient? Might it not, after all, simply be better to depart, to go anywhere else, rather than become involved in emotions which might easily be dissipated? True, he had just now committed himself. But need he stay committed?

"I must get back," he said, abruptly, rising from the bed. Cominthal, looking at him, seemed suddenly disturbed, less assured of him . . . and of himself.

"You are not going to forget again, are you? It's been too long—"

"No, no. I will see you again, soon. Tomorrow."

And now he paced in the dimness and the darkness, the smell of cool earth and damp grass in his nostrils, thinking, thinking. He passed some hours, thus solitary, then he returned to the house and fell quickly asleep.

But the quiet of the night did not extend into the daytime. Before an hour had passed after his getting up, he had a visitor. And a rather agitated visitor, too.

"Lord Tilionoth! You will honor me by tarrying long, I must hope," Tonoro said, still smooth in his mouth the polite phrases he had once so much relished—and not so long ago, either.

Abruptly, Tilionoth demanded, "Has Otho been to see you?"

"My lord? Who—?" He gestured towards a seat piled with smooth green cushions, but Tilionoth just made an annoyed movement, continued his disturbed walking quickly up and down.

"Otho. The man behind anything the Synod of Guardians —Othofarinal: There. Has he *been* here?"

The answer, and the truthful one, was that he had not. But the question, plus Tilionoth's obviously upset manner, rang warning signals in Tonoro's mind. What was this about the silver-haired and so-suave political leader and his possible visit here which could have so disturbed the young lord? Othofarinal had of course been here in the past, but it was obvious that the question must refer to the recent, indeed, the immediate past.

"Guardian Othofarinal has not honored the house at all lately. But there is nothing wrong, I must hope . . . ?"

Clearly, there was much wrong, but Lord Tilionoth's mind, never deep even when at rest, did not feel any irony or hypocrisy in his host's polite phrase. If anything, he was able to emerge from his agitation long enough to be a bit surprised that anyone was noticing that he was agitated at all.

"Anything wrong? Oh. . . . Why do you think . . . ? Well. . . . There may be, Tonorosant. I don't know. I don't know. One hesitates to— Look here," he said, abruptly, sitting himself down, suddenly, after all, and clasping his hands around one knee. "I'm asking you because you of your own free will did choose, you know, to ally yourself with us. With the Guardians, I mean. So you know that—it's been no secret, ever—my family have always been Guardian people and my becoming a Lord made no difference, everyone knows that. It's always been understood that our position entitled us to representation on both sides, but everyone knows— Well. Look here!" He got up and resumed his restless pacing, his young and rather vacantly handsome face glowing both with his emotions and the reflected coloring of his red robes.

"The other side, you do know, I must hope—the Lords— have of course been the top people for a long while now. I've not been the only one who's felt that things were past due for change. So I've been quite pleased to see all the activity in our camp this last while. And Otho's been in the thick of it all, behind everything. You do know that, I must hope. So when— But now— Well, Tonorosant, here it is: It's being said that he has sold us out. That he's actually been working to commit us on behalf of those who lack the Seven Signs. Exactly, the Lermencasi!"

Tonoro's heart lurched, then calmed, immediately. Things could not have stayed completely concealed forever. The rumor could not be a complete surprise to him.

"Shocks you, doesn't it?" Tilionoth asked. "Naturally. But if he hasn't been here lately, then of course you know nothing of. . . . It may be a complete lie. It *is* a complete lie, I must hope. Why, I would rather see the Lords rule forever, than that the Guardians do such a thing! Indeed, really, there's no other explanation for it: it must be a lie gotten up by the die-hard Lords, wouldn't you agree? A last-ditch attempt to keep their hold. . . . But such a vile way to go about it!" The young man was working himself into a passionate belief that his guess must be true. "As though any true Tarnisi for a moment would ever be guilty of such a thing. Well, as you know nothing about it I won't stay, I must go and see other people, track the slander down, crush it. Crush it!" His voice rose, his face began to work. In another moment he had gone.

A better method of disseminating the rumor than this one, it would have been hard to invent. Tonoro was himself quite disturbed. What would this disclosure, whether it was believed or not, do to the timetable for the take-over? Could it successfully be discredited, things proceed at the same pace according to the same schedule? Or would this unusual event in the Tarnisi scene-political result in the destruction of the power of the Guardians and perhaps even in their disappearance as a body? In which case, what would be his own situation, who was known to have involved himself with them?

The arrival of Cominthal found his cousin both nervous and concerned. "I want to talk to you about this matter of the Lermencasi," he began, at once.

"Talk, then." His face and voice were totally noncommittal.

Tonoro spoke of things, which, he said, hardly needed speaking of—the insufferable and sophisticated brutality of the Tarnisi, so much worse in both the long run and the short than the small-scale and primitive brutality of the Volanth. "You said that it can't go on, and you're only partly right. It *can*. But it isn't going to. There's that help from abroad that we both know about. Of course it isn't forthcoming to help *us*, principally. That's just a by-product of it. It would be nice to think that the sun would rise tomorrow on a Free and Equal Republic of Tarnis, with all three peoples friends and brothers. It isn't going to, though."

"No."

"The Lermencasi aren't moving in to liberate us or the Volanth. But their moving in will mean, if they recognize it or not, the eventual liberation of us *and* the Volanth. They'll want the Volanth for labor, true, but there's nothing wrong with labor as such. We've seen what living without laboring can do to a people, how corrupted and how decadent that can make them. The Volanth will be far better off working for the Lermencasi than they are now. And as for the Quasi? Us? We can be just as useful to the Lermencasi, but in a different way. As an intermediate group, I mean. The Quasi have less to discard—in the way of primitive habits —than the Volanth. Which means that they can learn faster. Our people can be to the Lermencasi more or less what the Pemathi here are to the Tarnisi . . . with the difference that this, Tarnis, is not just a place where we'll work for a while and then go away forever. This is our country, too. And sooner or later the time will come when we, or, I suppose rather, our children, will have learned how to govern it for and by themselves.

"It seems to me worth waiting for. The years of the Lermencasi rule can be regarded as the years of schooling. Let us sow their crops and reap them, and let them make their profits. It will be worth it to them, but it will be worth it to *us*, too."

Cominthal smiled, it was a thin and not a cheerful smile. "So now you have talked to me," he said, "about this matter of the Lermencasi."

"Yes. . . . I'll have some food brought, and—"

His cousin gestured the offer away. "Soon will be soon enough. I have something to talk about, too, you know. You will honor me by hearing me out, I must hope?" There was something chilling in this sudden return to the imitation of aristocratic courtesy. Tonoro only nodded. The late morning sun slotted in through the carven vertical slats of the window-blinds and now and then they shifted slightly with the breeze. Cominthal's face, half-masked, seemed to undergo a subtle transformation with each small movement in the flux of light and shadow.

"Let me see if I understand your notion of this help from abroad. With its help, instead of being outcasts, we'll be servants. Is that correct? And, if we are very good and learn our lessons well, our children . . . or, perhaps—eh?—our children's children . . . will be allowed the free use of their own country. The helpers from overseas will be nice and obliging and will just go away when they're asked to, ah? Well. You've lived among the foreign, cousin; you know them better than I. Will they go when they're asked? Ah?"

Tonoro said, "If they do not, they must be made to."

Cominthal's smile was rather warmer now. "That's right. If another people is ruling us and we don't want to be ruled by them, if they won't go, they must be made to go. We agree. But, then, cousin, why wait? I mean, you see: why let them in at all? If they never have our country, they'll never have to face giving it up. As for learning, well, we can hire our own teachers, don't you think? No, cousin, I'll tell you what it is about, this help from abroad: It will never have a span of our soil. It will arm us, we and the Volanth, cousin —they are our cousins, too—eh?—and we shall destroy the Tarnisi and then we'll rule ourselves. Not our children. We."

Tonoro said, "The Lermencasi will never do it."

And now the smile was very broad indeed. "The Lermencasi? No. That's true. They never will. But, you see, despite your great foreign *gorum,* there are still things which you don't know." The light shifted, advanced, receded. The smile was still broad, but it still had no warmth. "The foreign help I'm talking of isn't coming from the Lermencasi, ah, no.

"It's coming from the Bahon. . . ."

* * *

"You'll think about this," Cominthal had said, after eating, before departing. He had eaten heartily, hungrily, with only now and then a pretense of courtly courtesy when a servant entered with another course. "You'll think about it," he said, confidently, brightly.

"—But you won't talk about it."

And then he was gone.

The offices of the Commercial Deputation were maintaining their usual air of museum-like calm as Tonorosant walked down the corridors. The jewel-like settings seemed unreally beautiful. Could they actually have been the product of the same civilization which could—could? *had! did!*—sink so suddenly and so frequently and so utterly into savage coercion? And was it actually, need it actually be doomed: that same civilization which in them and by them demonstrated its title to be so called? He found his arms and legs were beginning to tremble. He walked faster. Then he slowed again. He did not know by whom he was likely to be seen, and it would not do to give his notice, by openly displayed agitation, that he knew more than he was generally known to know.

As he approached the screen of the Deputy's office he heard a familiar voice. "My dear Mothiosant, how much I sympathize with you . . . how exceedingly tedious your conscript duties can become."

The Pemathi clerk rose at Tonorosant's entrance; he waved the man back to his seat and passed on in.

"It is true, Sarlamat, but I will not remain in this place of duty forever, I must hope. These bothersome contracts, for example—well, and is it my fault if there is not enough resin? Can I secrete it myself, like a tree? For—"

His voice ceased and his face changed, pretense dropping from it, as he saw Tonoro. Sarlamat swerved about to look at him. There was a moment's silence. Then Mothiosant continued, "For if there is not enough resin to fulfill the terms of the contract, thus it is, and indeed, what can I or any of us do? Boy!"

"Master?"

"You may go out to your food-chop, now."

A polite mumble from the clerk, slight noises of departure, and then again silence. Sarlamat's face now looked neither jovial nor ironic. Insofar as it bore a discernible expression, the expression was one of slight fatigue. Mothiosant, on the other hand, looked keyed-up and intent. He held out his hand now, palm up, fingers moving impatiently.

"Here is a hypothetical situation which may just possibly, if we can resolve its problems, throw some light on an actual situation," Tonoro said. Mothiosant at once became a trifle wary. But still his fingers moved restlessly, demanding his visitor to talk.

"Suppose there is a world called, oh, not Orinel, its name would not matter, but very much like Orinel in its physical and its social make-up. Unlike a number of worlds, this one's population is not confined to one ethnos or one kith —or race, or people; choose your own preferred term—nor has it only one planetary governance. The nations and people it does have are of varying types of social structure. Some are heavily industrialized, some are actively commercial, some are so overpopulated that they have slid downwards. Others are not only underpopulated but rather isolated and are still largely what we may call 'backward' in most things.

"Let's concern ourselves with one of these in our hypothetical situation. Culturally and economically, this nation is not merely backward; it is archaic. Let's pretend it's Tarnis. Its potential as a producer-nation has not barely begun to be exploited. But the potential is there.

"Do you follow me, my brothers' brothers?"

Sarlamat's mouth had tightened just a bit. He was rotating his left forefinger between his right forefinger and thumb, around and around and back and forth, and gazing at it with a slight frown of concentration. Mothiosant's expression had not changed at all. "Go on," he said. His tone said, *Be quick*. His own fingers repeated their own urgent motion.

"Now two other factors enter this hypothetical picture. For one thing, every land has its laws. For another, there are always men who break or who are accused of breaking these laws. And who, in consequence, wish to flee from punishment. Let us assume the existence of an organization set up to capitalize on the needs of such men—an organization set up for the sole purpose—ostensibly—of commercializing on that need, of enabling these men to disguise themselves physically and mentally. Of enabling them, for example, to come to the island-nation which—hypothetically, of course—we've agreed to call Tarnis. What shall we call this imaginary organization? Shall we call them the Craftsmen?"

One looked at him still, and one still looked at his own hands only, and neither one spoke.

Tonorosant continued. "I said, 'ostensibly. . . .' Suppose this organization was not after all in business to make a profit out of its clandestine activities directly. Suppose, in fact, that the factual cost of its services were such that the fees charged, however high, could not cover them. Suppose, in further fact, that it was actually but one arm of an ambitious and gigantic commercial combine which was underwriting its expenses as a form of investment. That these men were never intended to be made free, but were intended to serve the aims of the organization, wherever they might go. But this is perhaps too large a subject for our hypothetical discussion. Let's confine it to our one hypothetical nation of Tarnis, and—again, for the purposes of our discussion only, of course—let us refer to this entire organization as . . . say . . . Commerce-Lermencas.

"The aim was to subvert the social structure and the governance of the imaginary Tarnis, and make it the servant of Lermencas. The vast Outlands would be subjected to scientific cultivation and agriculture and arboriculture would no longer be limited to the crude methods locally employed. And the Volanth, for example, would cease to be outlaws and would become . . . oh, various possibilities exist . . . employees . . . serfs. . . . Whichever, they would be better off than now.

"Now. Suppose that the ruling class of our imaginary Tarnis becomes aware, at least in part, of these plans for them. And suppose that another nation does, as well—"

They looked up, then, abruptly, the both of them.

"What other nation?"

"Again—hypothetically and nothing more—say—oh . . . the Bahon."

Mothiosant: "Why would the Bahon—"

Sarlamat: " 'Why would the Bahon' is not the question. There are many reasons why the Bahon would. The question is, '*Are* the Bahon—?' " His full lips drew back from his even teeth. "An end to this nonsense, Jerred Northi. Your Bahon are not hypothetical. You are not conjecturing, you are speaking from actual knowledge. *What do you know about the Bahon's intentions at the present moment?"*

He said, "The Craftsmen did not serve me for nothing and I am not going to serve the Craftsmen for nothing."

"No one expects you to," Sarlamat said, immediately. "By learning what you have learned, whatever it is, you've immediately become worth more to us than the whole amount you have cost us. Naturally, you have a price—and naturally, we'll pay it."

Mothiosant nodded instant and vigorous assent. They both listened, with total absorption and (so it seemed) total commitment. This remained unchanged even after Tonoro had finished speaking, as though, perhaps, his voice gave forth an echo which only they could hear . . . and which they dared not miss.

The Commercial Deputy shifted slightly, sighed slightly. He glanced at Sarlamat, who said, "I must confess that we were not expecting a price of that sort. An end to all offenses against Quasi and Volanth—that would be inevitable, eventually, in any case. But you want, am I correct, an immediate end? Full equality? A massive educational program to fit them for this, but this not to wait upon the completion of that? Inducements and concessions . . . yes. . . . I have it all, now. And I think—" he turned to his associate.

"I think it can be done," Mothiosant said. "Of course, we must get it confirmed; you would hardly want to take our word for it alone. Can this evening be soon enough? Then you will see us here again. Meanwhile, is not our almost certain conviction that it can be done enough to persuade you that you should tell us—"

"No."

The Deputy's mouth twisted. He put his hand out as he spoke, it stayed, arrested, and he looked at it as though surprised at what he saw. Sarlamat got up. "Let's waste no time, then. But just think of this: You lived most of your life in a world where more hungered than did not, and more died than survived. This island-land of Tarnis has lain on its richness and its riches like a toothless dog. It can produce enough to feed every hungry mouth in Pemath. Surely you aren't naive enough to believe that the Bahon are concerned with the welfare of the Pemathi or the Tarnisi? Of the Quasi or Volanth? It must be made absolutely clear to you: Anything which Baho does vis-a-vis Lermencas is done as part of a power struggle. If we succeed here, of course it will advance us throughout the world! And the only thing about our plans here which concerns Baho is that we must be defeated in order that *Baho* is to be advanced throughout the world! Now go, and we will see you here this evening to confirm your demands."

* * *

Tulan Tarolioth shook his head. His hands trembled, and, indeed, his whole trim, small body quivered with restrained emotion. Atoral, by his side, placed her hand on his shoulder.

"My whole life since I became a man has been devoted to securing justice for the wild people," he said, his voice frequently escaping control. "What I have suffered, I and my house, you do not know and you will never know, I must hope. But I have never lost my faith that those who have the Seven Signs will become worthy of the traditional ethics, and grant that justice. Only last week I spoke of this to a young man, one of the most hopeful young men we have, and he admitted to me that he was impressed by what I told him on that point. You may know him: the Lord Tilionoth."

Tonoro controlled his face and voice. "I do know him," he said. How far the old man had retreated from reality, to accept what could have been no more than polite commonplaces for awakening conviction! Lord Tilionoth, of all possible people!

"And today he returned to tell me that it has been charged

that the Lermencasi have agents thick as flies among the Volanth and that they have promised to drive us into the sea and divide our lands up and give them to the Volanth!"

"Rumors, Tulan—mere lying rumors that you cannot believe, I must hope—"

The old man's face quivered with the force of his shaking his head. "Rumors, once raised, never vanish without trace. This entire cause, to which I have devoted my life—my *life!* —is now tainted. I hope not forever. I must hope not forever. I must hope that my name counts for something. I am too old to begin all over again."

He paused, striving to keep from weeping. He seemed too old, at that moment, to do anything much more. His sincerity, his devotion to the cause of justice for the Volanth was without question, although the success of his attempts had been almost nil. Still, still, his name *did* count for something. He was respected, he had some followers, he had many friends. His absurd attempts to base a pro-Volanth philosophy upon the ancient tenets of the Tarnisi ethic might not be so utterly absurd in a different sort of situation. Suppose that the Volanth were forcibly emancipated. Might not a comforting and familiar-sounding set of lies provide the only way of accepting the situation for the Tarnisi? And thus avoid the perhaps otherwise inevitable appeal to bloodshed. . . .

But things were moving so quickly, now. Things were moving too quickly, now. Here in this dusty old room, filled with bas-reliefs of ancestral tulans and unpublished pamphlets, ancient books and general clutter—even here the rushing present had entered, and was now driving all before it and upsetting and overturning all. How the fact of Lermencasi involvement had gotten out, he, Tonoro ("Jerred Northi," they'd called him just a while ago; he'd almost forgotten Jerred Northi) did not know. And then that fool, Tilionoth, taking time off from his preoccupation with spearthrowers and violent sex, had somehow gotten hold of a fragment of the fact and gone flitting from place to place like a demented insect, distorting and allowing to be distorted the rumor as he proceeded on his heedless, dangerous, and by now probably deadly way.

Tonorosant had come here to Atoral's home in hopes of sounding out her father about the possibility of enlisting his support to make as smooth as might be the change which was inevitable. He had thought that, properly presented, his appeal could not fail. Now he found it could not succeed. The mere mention of foreign intervention had almost unhinged the tulan; he would now not just lean backwards, he was almost standing on his head, to make it quite clear that he and his faction had, had had, and would have nothing to do with it. Too, and understandably, he had been terrified almost witless by the suggestion that the landed aristocracy would not only be reduced to the status of lacklanders, but would see their lands divided up among the Volanth. Tulan Tarolioth would, without question, give his life to see that "the wild people" were given justice—justice, yes: but not given the Tarnisi lands! He would gladly give the Volanth his own life, but he had never contemplated giving them his own land!

So, now, he barely understood what purpose Tonoro had in coming, had barely given him time or leave to explain anything of his purpose. Clearly, it would be vain to remain.

"Insofar as I have disturbed you and the peace of your august house," Tonoro said, bowing, and preparing to leave, "you will forgive me, I must hope." He looked up at Atoral, slightly raised his eyebrows. Would she come with him? But she shook her head; though the gesture was slight, her expression was firm. So, then, he, Tonoro, would have to see his way through this, muddle his way, fight, dig, claw, whatever it was, his way through this . . . without her . . . alone.

Once more he bowed. Suddenly the tulan held up his hand. A hope flared in Tonoro's mind. The old man came forward, again shaking his head, this time in evident self-reproach. "The cause is too important," he said. "It is too important for me to allow you to leave without— No, my sister's child. Ah, no. No, no." He stopped and put his hand to his forehead. Then his face cleared. "Just so," he said. "Allow me to present you with a small pamphlet which I happen to have written on the sacred subject we have just been discussing. It will interest you, I must hope. . . ."

* * *

The countryside and prospects of the not-very-distant city had perhaps never looked lovelier than they did now in the light of the latening afternoon. The low, spreading houses of the estates and all their beautifully kept grounds, the curving lines of trees which emphasized rather than concealed the sinuous lines of the lovely river, greensward and copses of flowering trees; and, in the town, the glittering spires and the occasional crowns of trees rising higher than the garden walls, with their hints and reminders: golden gardens, sunken gardens, night gardens. Flights of birds circled overhead, as though their song signaled their own pleasure in the sight.

But Tonoro felt a heaviness which was physical as well as mental and emotional. He had one more call to make before the evening, and as he proceeded in his trim float, the same thoughts passed through his mind over and over again, circling like the birds. But without singing.

The Lermencasi planned to exploit the Volanth, but the Volanth (and the Quasi as well) would eventually learn enough from them to replace them. The Tarnisi would be weakened by the Lermencasi takeover, and this was a good thing: gradually they would be obliged to adapt and improve their attitude towards the "lesser" peoples of the country. When the time arrived, the Tarnisi would have to ally themselves with Quasi and Volant for conjoint action against the alien Lermencasi.

But if the Lermencasi accepted his, Tonoro's plan, then all would be accelerated. No one need fight anybody. No one *need*—

Which did not mean that no one *would*—

Suppose, though, that the Bahon plan was the winning one, with its utterly abrupt change, and no chance of gradual adjustment. Likely, the Tarnisi would be utterly crushed, either destroyed or driven into exile. Could the Volanth manage the required upward climb . . . in a vacuum? Would it not be inevitable that they must then submit to be ruled by the inexperienced if somewhat more sophisticated Quasi —who moreover, in most cases, also loathed them? Might this not be just as bad?

Then, too: Tonoro himself. And Atoral. Sooner or later he must tell her that he himself was a Quasi. And what then? What then, what then, what then?

Still his thoughts circled and circled till they seemed to have taken on physical shape and form. It was only then that he blinked and looked and realized that he was hemmed in by at least a dozen other floats. Down— Down— They gestured to him to put down; gestured with hands containing charge-throwers. And he obeyed. Stepping out of his own craft, he said, "The answer, then, is 'No', Mothiosant?"

"The answer is 'No,' " Mothiosant said, as they quickly

bound Tonoro and placed him in another float. Getting in beside him, he repeated, "The answer is 'No.' "

"Then you don't wish to learn what the Bahon plan is."

Mothiosant sighed. "Really, as Sarlamat pointed out after you left, the Bahon plan became obvious the moment you mentioned them. After all, there are only a certain number of possibilities. An outright invasion is out of the question —Orinel politics have passed that stage long ago. Subversion, conversion, disaffection: these are the only possibilities. Well—they could not have been working on the Tarnisi: *we* were working on the Tarnisi. It is a sum in simple subtraction and one easily made—you made it easier by mentioning the Quasi and Volanth."

"You over-simplify."

"And you, poor former pirate, you play for time. Be quiet."

Quiet he was. But Mothiosant had, after all, stated things rather clearly. *There are only a certain number of possibilities.* Sarlamat, far the keener of the two, would have himself stayed quiet.

Only a certain number of possibilities.

Below him the land slipped slowly into darkness. Lovely land, forever vexed with unlovely deeds. The Craftsmen could not now proceed with their former intentions; there was not time; they might not know when the Bahon would move; therefore they themselves had to move fast. They could not be working or intend to work with the Volanth and the Quasi: the Bahon were doing this. They could not intend a compromise: Tonoro had proposed this and they had— obviously—rejected his proposal. Moreover, the rapidity with which they had moved against him was an indication that they dared not allow him at large. And therefore it was clear that they themselves intended to move rapidly.

The technique of world-polity prohibited their moving nakedly and openly by themselves. And this left but one possibility.

The Craftsmen, under whatever guise, were going to reveal the Bahon plan to the Tarnisi. And then, with them, move against both the Quasi and the Volanth.

CHAPTER ELEVEN

The floats swerved around and turned their backs on the waning colors of the sunlight and angled down into a walled enclosure in the one single port area which the Tarnisi grudgingly allowed. Its massive doors at once identified it as one of the long-abandoned old forts dating from the days of the wars of the Lords and the Guardians. However, it had been kept up in a state of repair, and not a blade of grass grew in the vast yard where once swordsmen and spearsmen had practiced.

"Be cautious, Tonorosant. Things will soon be settled in proper order. We are not vengeful, you know. Afterwards, I am sure we can find an excellent place for you in our plans. Or, if you prefer, you can go—anywhere you like. So don't jeopardize your future." Mothiosant gave instructions to the men waiting; then, in another moment, he and the others were gone. For a long moment, Tonoro, watching, saw the vessels climb and wheel and then vanish.

He had had some notion and hope that he would . . . that he might . . . be placed under Pemathi guard. And that then, being able to speak their language, he might somehow contrive their aiding his escape. But the sight of those who were actually to have him in custody—either genuine Tarnisi or Craftsmen-made imitators like himself—was really no surprise. *Jerred Northi*, Sarlamat called him that morning. And *You, poor pirate*, Mothiosant said when they captured him. So: they knew who he was, knew, too, his background in Pemath. And were taking no chances.

Once inside, the mystery of the place's non-neglect was at the instant explained. —Explained by the combined scents, smells, odors, reeks and just plain stinks of sundry staple items ranging from timber to dried fish. The fort had been restored of its neglect and made to do duty as a warehouse. Mothiosant, as Commercial Deputy, would have the place completely in his hands; other Tarnisi would no more think of going there than to a charnel house.

"Might as well get these off," one man, evidently in charge, said, stooping and grunting as he removed the cords. "You're not in a float now, you can kick out all you want, and it won't upset a thing."

He paused at the smaller door next to the massive one and made a mock bow devoid of malice. "After you—"

The warehouse seemed to contain nothing but much-mingled smells; Tonoro was reminded of the scene at Compound Ten after the conclusion of the last "war" in the Outlands, the plunder of foodstuffs and staple tradestuffs being stacked in place by the forced labor of the Volanth. Perhaps that very produce had passed through this place en route overseas. The slits and slots in the thick walls were now quite useless for illumination, but light-units had been set up and shed their faintly orange glow on the thick, worn slabs of the floor—floor which had been swept quite clean by the Pemathi after the last clearance, not because the Pemathi were compulsively neat but because even the sweepings would have had a money value, however slight. Once, as he passed under a heavy old archway his eye was caught by a glimmer of color still adhering to an ancient wall-painting done, probably, to while away the more peaceful hours of some forgotten siege: a Tarnisi warrior cutting off the head of a spear-transfixed mass of hair doubtless intended for a vanquished Volanth.

Much had changed in the interval of centuries. But not the Tarnisi character.

After the archway, a ramp. After the ramp, a corridor. After the corridor, an enormous room. They started to cross it; it seemed to him that they were giving him covert, amused looks. He barely had time to wonder why when something seemed to move, convulsively, inside of him. He made a startled noise and a startled movement. The men laughed, stopped.

"There, you see, fellow," the man in charge said, pointing down at a cable which lay circling around on the floor; "you step or jump—or even, I guess, *fly!*—over that, coming in, and it feels quite funny. Doesn't it? Didn't really hurt, though, did it? Just feels damned queer. Coming *in*. But. Don't you try it going *out*. That's, indeed, the most genuinely warm advice I could give you. It won't just feel peculiar going out. It will hurt like all anguish, you see. And what is beyond question much more to the point: it won't *work*. You can't get out. *You*. Not us. Try it . . . if you like. . . . No? Then, good."

The cable had an odd look, somewhat like quicksilver, somewhat like . . . something he had not a name for. He followed them on into the interior of the great circle formed by the cable. Behind, the light-units slowly, softly turned themselves off. Ahead was a rather hastily improvised, so it looked, cross between a lounge pavilion and a levy bivouac. "Eat here . . . sleep there . . . sanitary stall . . . and all on an if-and-when you like basis. Now, either excuse us or join us, for we're about to be busy."

He snapped his fingers, there was a quick taking of seats, and, from a microtrans which Tonoro had not till now noticed, a 3D performance in full vigor of sound and smell and action burst out upon them. It was musical, it was Lermencasi, it did not greatly interest him. But it evidently greatly interested the men. Probably all or most of them were Lermencasi, too: Commerce-L. might not mind at all making the Craftsmen's services available to those who might have gotten on the wrong side of power in Lermencas . . . provided, probably, that they hadn't gotten on the wrong side of Commerce-L.

It was the first 3D show he'd seen since leaving Pemath; although he'd sounded out the possibilities, the chances of getting permission to import microtranses had never looked good. This was one "foreign toy" on which Tarnis still frowned: Still intent as the Tarnisi were on keeping out, en masse, those who "lacked the Seven Signs," they had no desire to admit their images—not merely into their country, but into their very homes. It occurred to Tonoro that this setup here in the old warehouse-fort might have been arranged originally not as a makeshift jail but as a sort of clandestine theater.

It was a long, *long* performance, with a cast (evidently) of thousands; dazed by the noise and clamor even after it had ceased for intermission, Tonoro stayed in his seat as the others got up, stretched, visited the stall, made themselves drinks or snacks. His reaction on hearing the voice shout, *"Down flat! Down flat!"* was instinctive. He obeyed. Went down, went flat. Wondered that no one else did. Realized that the voice had shouted in Pemathi . . . that, seemingly, no one else here understood. Someone had asked something in a voice of alarmed confusion. There was a thudding, cracking sound—no: not one sound, several. Now, at last, the others went down—one of them, screaming. Cautiously, Tonoro moved his head. Voices were echoing. There was blood. The others were down, all right. But not exactly flat down. In awkward heaps, at grotesque angles. The man who had been screaming now began to sob.

"Tonoro!" The voice echoed.

"Tonoro?" It called again and echoed again.

He cried, "Here!"—and then, having wisely or not wisely thus committed himself, he got up.

Confusion was, for a while, worse confounded. He shouted for them (whoever they were) not to cross the cable. But some already had. Some tried to cross back. That was nasty. There was a hurried search for the switch to activate all the light-units, the man with the shattered arm was—somehow—persuaded to bethink himself of this information, and then to reveal it. The others seemed all to be dead. . . .

He had guessed who and what it might be even before the orange glow sprang up all around and he saw Cominthal and many men standing back from the cable. Volanth were among them; he had realized it must be so when he saw the smooth stones. And saw the crushed skulls. He was somewhat regretful that the man in charge was dead, though it was not accurate to say that he had liked him. But, given time and other circumstances, he might have. No time to dwell on that. To the man now moaning on his knees he said, rapidly, "The cable. How is it crossed safely?" The man wept in the grief of pain and the shock of fear; shook his head.

"If they don't get in soon they may break the other arm, you know—"

"Belts! It's the belts!" he cried in a frenzy of concern. The belts—he pointed to his waist. Quickly, Tonoro stripped three of them from the heedless dead, ran to the cable. They felt rather heavier than they should, but, looping one around himself, he had no time to reflect on what that might mean. The old, groined roof sent back the echo of his pounding feet, as it had sent back in days of old the noise of the captains and the shouting of ancient wars. He girded two of the men inside the circle, and together they crossed over. He felt no more than a twinge, stripped off his and the others' belts, passed them across to those still inside. One, a middle-aged Volanth with a strong face, evidently not understanding, failed to put on the belt and—even as Tonoro and the others cried out warning—passed safely over with it held in his hand. Evidently it was all in the belt, and not in how or where it was worn.

"Let's get away from here," Cominthal said—then added a word or two in the Volanth tongue. The last man out nodded, put his hand in the pouch by his side, hefted the stone a moment, then threw back his arm, gauging with his eye the man with the shattered arm.

Tonoro caught hold of the thrower's hand. Said, "No."

Cominthal said, "We can't take him with us and we can't have him getting out to sound an alarm. Really, if he merits a kindness, this is it."

But, in the end, they didn't do him that kindness. They merely took his belt away. They left him there among the bodies, the blood, drinks spilled and unspilled, food scattered and unscattered. He clutched his hand and stared. And, just as they passed from sight, they heard the 3D drama spring back into gaudy life, saw it burst into bouncy sight once more.

The intermission was over.

* * *

"How did you learn Pemathi?"

"I learned all of it I wanted to—one phrase. How? I asked."

"How did you know where I was?"

Cominthal's mouth stretched briefly into a one-sided smile. "I never let you out of someone's sight since we last met.... Tell me it all, my uncle's son."

He listened, grim, intent, to his cousin's account of what had passed between him and the two emissaries of Lermencas, and to his, Tonoro's, conjectures of what would now have to be the Lermencasi plans. " 'Move immediately against the Quasi and the Volanth,' " he repeated. "Yes— but when? How much 'immediately'? Now? Tomorrow? We have to know. I am sure that you are right so far. So be right a bit further. You know the foreign minds. Eh?"

Tonoro said, "I can extrapolate, make educated surmises. I can't make *gorum,* you know. I can't prophesy. But.... Now? I don't think quite now. In order for them to overcome the suspicion and prejudice the Tarnisi have toward foreigners they'll have to devise something very huge and special in the way of lies. Otherwise neither Lords nor Guardians nor anyone else will consent to Lermencasi participation. It won't matter that those two, Sarlamat and Mothiosant, and the other Craftsmen clients here, are still posing as Tarnisi. In order to wipe out Quasi and Volanth—".

Cominthal seized his wrist. "You think that? Wipe us out?"

"As near as they can."

"Who'll be their slaves, then?"

"Labor? They can import it, by contract. Pemathi, perhaps. Why not?"

His cousin said, "Go on."

They had left the old fort-warehouse, the Volanth carefully retrieving their thrown stones for future use; this time they proceeded through the gates and not by notched log-ladders as they had entered. The present moment found them far enough away, in the sub-basement of a mean inn catering exclusively to lacklanders . . . most of whom, in this case, were actually Quasi who had succeeded in "passing." Broken furniture and rubbish of all sorts clogged the crowded cellar. A gilded mirror with a crack in it lay propped in such a way that its reflection wavered and trembled incessantly. The light was very low and dim, the switch lay in Cominthal's hand so that at the first alarm he could plunge the room in darkness.

"It's appropriate, I suppose," Tonoro went on, "that foreign assistance will be used by the Tarnisi against the Volanth. They loath and fear the foreigners—but they loath and fear the Volanth even more. So their most basic bigotry will be their undoing. . . . Which would do us no good. No— I can think of only one thing which would force the Tarnisi into a foreign alliance. And that's for them to get a hint of the truth."

"That we're plotting against them?"

"Yes. It would send them so near mad with rage and fear that the Lermencasi could lack human form and not just the Seven Signs and they'd still go along with them. But they can't work up a presentation immediately. As yet they have no proof in hand about the Bahon and they certainly won't want to admit the intentions and endeavors of the Lermencasi —Besides, the fact that a trickle of the truth about an indirect link between Lermencas and the Guardians has gotten out is going to make things even more difficult. So they'll have to take a while to fix up a fake case with fragments of fact.

"The question is, *How long a while?* It's a qualified immediacy, and that's as close as I can say. And all else that I can say is: They are going to move fast and therefore *we* are going to have to move faster."

Cominthal got to his feet. His reflection danced and

trembled in the broken mirror. "We have already begun to move," he said.

* * *

Bishdar Shronk made growling noises as he listened. From time to time he turned to the maps and charts and then returned, restlessly, still growling, to his seat. Bearlike man, huge of head and trunk, seamed and weathered face, abrupt, loud, suspicious. Bishdar Shronk. Bahon.

"A bad time," he said, and growled. "We hadn't thought to have to move this soon. The ground is not prepared for it, the people are not prepared—either here or at home. Before—" He flung his bristly paw of a hand at the charts, the maps. "Before, it was a matter of preparing the ground. A long process. Working with the oppressed to overthrow the oppressors. A certain number involved, no more. Tarnis is not greatly populated." He grunted, flipped his hand back, shifted his bulk.

"But now!" he exclaimed, in a low roar. "Now Lermencas enters in! Or, Commerce-Lermencas, which is the same thing. . . . The United Syndicates of Baho are not surprised, we knew it was inevitable. Not content with their illegal seizure of the Archipelago of Ran— But I am sure you know their wretched history. The problem is *now*. The United Syndicates cannot yet fully mobilize our forces. Also, present planetary polity here on Orinel rules out open involvement of one nation in the affairs of another. What, then—"

He mused a moment, growling. Then he thumped his fists on the table. "Everything indicates that we must make a lightning move—arm the Volanth—hurl them at the ruling class—destroy the power of that class before Lermencas can move, itself. But—"

"But with what would one arm the Volanth?" Tonoro broke in.

"Exactly . . . rrrr. . . . With what? Leeri? Fire-charges? How soon could they be trained?"

Cominthal began a passionate argument about arming the Quasi instead. "Time would be wasted trying to train the Volanth in the use of modern armament," he concluded. "They're a primitive horde, they hunt by slinging rocks at small game. But the Quasi—"

Bishdar Shronk growled a negative. "Too few, too few," he said. "Also, the Volanth, besides being so much more numerous, are the more notoriously oppressed. The polity of the situation requires that argument for support be on the side of the majority of the populace. Everyone knows about the Volanth. If we are to act, it must be for them and with them and through them. The Quasi are a fraction. If only there were more time—education would logically begin with that fraction, it forms a link between two worlds—but time there is not, and even if we put fire-arms in the hands of every adult Quasi, it would not be enough."

And Tonoro said, "Not firearms and not the Quasi." It was as though he were thinking aloud. "But hands, yes. Hands and arms—" He rose, his heart filled with a necessary terror which was not devoid of exaltation. He spoke and they listened. He spoke and they looked each at the other. He finished speaking. They nodded. And they began to move, faces both animated and grave.

"It might do it," said Bishdar Shronk, making yet another trip to the maps. "It should do it," he amended. He nodded slowly, deeply, his blunt mouth pursed. "I'll send the signal—"

Cominthal's body slouched as though he were about to fall, but it was not weakness which posed him. He straightened up. He glared. " 'Might,' " he repeated. " 'Should' . . . . You. You two. Listen. If it fails, one of you can go back to Baho and the other one to Pemath—or anywhere else. But I have no place to go. None of us have any place to go. Except here, *here*. We're fighting for our lives and no one is going to give us a choice of surrender, you know that? 'Might.' 'Should.' Don't say those words, do you hear? Don't say them!

"It *must* do it!"

* * *

The Pemathi on duty in Tarnis Port—which was a port, pure and simple, and not a city to itself as ports elsewhere so often were—had processed the incoming Lermencasi freighter with his usual care, but with a shade more interest than usual. For one thing, it was not a scheduled freighter; this was most unusual—in fact, it had never happened before to him—but the clerk of the Commercial Deputy had advised him, (unofficially, but most sincerely) that there were certain to be an unknown number of such at any time for the present. And told him, straightforwardly, to make no fuss. Something out of the ordinary was clearly going on, but the port duty man did not much care. In less than a year he was due to go on leave; his mind was on the piece of ground in the Hills of Tor which his brother was going to buy for him—with his, the duty man's money—if he liked its looks. Retirement was ten years off, but this would be time enough to build the house so that it would be ready and waiting when the time to dwell in it came. It would be built in the old-fashioned, rural Pemathi way, by the entire family and most of the clan, whenever there was time to spare from other work. Months might go by before the cellar was all dug out. Weeks would likely elapse between the laying of one course of stone and the laying of another. The brother would on occasion disburse a little money to buy a little food or drink or *kip*—a very little—for the pleasure of the builders. He might take a score of fortnights to cheapen the price of a beam. But the house would be done in time enough. The owner would not have paid any of his kinsmen a ticky for labor and it would not occur to him that he should. And any of his kinsmen who desired to would simply move in to share the house with him and it would not occur to him that they should not.

So, thus preoccupied with pleasant dreams, he processed the incoming freighter, punching the proper keys and saying the proper words and watching her settle in the proper berth, and watching the proper unloading mechanisms rise into place, the task of refueling commence simultaneously and in proper order. There were no freight floats in waiting, and this caused him some mild and momentary wonder, but he supposed they would be along in sufficient time. They were; he ceased entirely to concern himself in the matter. In another year he was going home on leave; he scanned the sequence in his mind. The voyage in a companionably crowded dormitory section. The pause at the Double Ports of Pemath for various forms of sensual exercise. The trip upcountry via river—slow, but cheap . . . and pleasant—the welcoming. A banquet at his expense for the clan elders; prestige maintained by having three dishes for everyone; thrift maintained by these being moderately small dishes. All predetermined. The only open question was marriage. Should—

"What vessel is that out there, boy?"

Not a flicker passed over the duty operator's pale, freckled face to indicate either that he resented having his pleasant meditations interrupted or that he was surprised by the sudden and unexpected appearance of the Commercial Deputy.

"Master, Lermencas ship bring freight-chop."

"Yes, I can *see* that. But what—"

The Pemathi had observed that Mothiosant was playing neither his languid, indifferent public role nor the crisp, efficient private one known to the Pemathi grapevine. The man was—and this was new—nervous, agitated. But the operator had anticipated the next question, tapped a key, pointed to the photoscan, prepared to interpret the sequence of symbols and numbers if the Commercial Deputy were going to pretend he could not. But the quick knowing way the latter eyed the scan, his mutter of "general cargo," showed that he wasn't.

"Well. I'm going down. Switch on for me," he said, and was gone.

The operator permitted himself one yawn, watched through the transparent walls as the Deputy seated himself on the moving overhead, switched it on, watched it glide down the ramp. It was not essential that he marry on his visit. Should, however, his clan find a girl sufficiently dowered or sufficiently well-connected or sufficiently comely, should the astromancers observe the connection to be fortuitous, he might do so. . . . *What* was the Deputy doing, standing up recklessly like that in his moving seat? *Why* was he waving his hands? Climbing the barrier to the opposite side? Did he mean he wanted the up-track switched on? Probably. The operator tapped the switch. Something was out of the ordinary. Which meant, almost certainly, that something was wrong. He watched a moment more, then gave a deep sigh, slid to the floor, crawled into the windowless inner chamber adjacent, closed the door, got under the table. This was all rather disappointing, but it was of course predestined. It remained questionable whether predestination was particular (in which case, precautions were useless) or merely general. At any rate, he had already sent his last quarter's savings abroad. And on deposit in the clan shrine were his nail clippings, hair combings, and the requisite five drops of blood.

Part of him, at least, would receive proper burial in his native land.

* * *

Tonoro almost felt himself to be Jerred Northi again altogether. It would be good if he could have had his old crews here with them, but at least he had not forgotten his old skill at organizing illicit ventures. The present one had something in common with tow-tapping, although of course it was both more dangerous and more—incomparably much more—important. It had been obvious to him, for example, that a Bahon-built freighter would not do for this first trip in—afterwards, perhaps, concealment might not be necessary. To his surprise, this had not been equally obvious to Bishdar Shronk and Cominthal, though they admitted the point immediately. Inexperienced entirely at this sort of thing, they had then fretted because pirating a Lermencasi bottom might arouse instant suspicion; it was he who had pointed out that one could be chartered at once without difficulty or question at any one of a score of ports. And he it was, too, who had arranged for the freight floats to be on hand to pick up this first cargo; that took even more conniving and contriving. . . . It was *quite* useful to have been a tow-tapper. And to know the thousand and half a thousand ways of obtaining Pemathi assistance without giving public notice of the fact.

The floats came down along the slot, paused, received their mechanically unloaded cargo, continued down along the slot to its end, and were then off under their own power each to a different destination. It would take complete mobilization devoted to that one purpose alone for the Tarnisi to find even some of them—and long before that could have been done they would have unloaded and left. Unloaded: under the dripping trees of some northern forest. Unloaded: on the threshing field of some hamlet of thatched hovels. Unloaded: on an island in the river. In a high place surrounded by marsh. The shanty suburbs of a city. Unloaded under the slow-melting stars and the moonless night sky of Orinel.

The smell of fuel was in his nostrils, nothing but the small sound of the machinery and an occasional whisper in his ears, his mind preoccupied with thought of Atoral . . . surely she would be safe? Surely her father's long pro-Volanth views were universally known, his recent, sudden, about-face not yet common knowledge. Surely his house would be spared. Tonoro had spoken of it more than once to Cominthal, each time obtained an impatient assurance. So, now, he was trying to put the matter out of his mind.

Seconds afterwards he realized that he had been aware of the figure seated on the moving overhead, had even observed it suddenly stand up and peer over the side. But he had not been concerned with it until it cried out the first syllables of his name. Then it was that the spell of the night and the mechanical motions of the scene and his preoccupied thoughts was broken. The unloading went on as before, but nothing else did. The man there, forward and above, was Mothiosant. Did he know, then? Voices shouted, feet came pounding. He knew now. *Had* he known? No, else he would not be here alone? *Was* he alone? No time to reflect, consider, plan. Time only to act. Mothiosant tried to leap over the barrier dividing the up-track from the down-, fell back. A fire-charge wooshed and snapped. He got to his feet, began to climb over. Another charge. Another. His leg remained in view on the barrier, as though he had detached it in his struggles, but the cry of pain following the next charge showed that he hadn't. And all the while he kept shouting something.

Tonoro alone had noticed the subtle change in the mechanical sounds from the overhead. He now gave the quick orders which intercepted a case from the unloading, opened it quickly and carefully, picked out the black, egglike objects, passed one to one of the Volanth who had appeared from out of the shadows, signaled for and obtained sudden silence.

"He is going *that* way now . . . he's dropped down so that we can't see him or even his seat from here. You'll have to gauge by the sound. Can you?"

The Volanth's confident grin distended his hairy mouth. He cocked his head, hefted the object in his hand, was for a second all intent attention (thus must he have listened for the rustling or perhaps even the breathing of small creatures hidden in the thickets) and in one swift movement had thrown it. They saw it rise, curve, descend. Heard the *crump* which followed. Heard the machinery grind to a halt. Saw that portion of the overhead dissolve into dust and saw the dust sift to the ground in the orange glow of the light-units. For a moment there was no sound save the satisfied one the thrower made in his throat, deep.

For now Tonoro knew for sure that he had indeed found the ideal weapon with which to arm the Volanth. Of its history he knew very little; the process of self-education in his case had scarcely allowed for research into the subject of subatomic particles. But this much he had known—the only type of atomic weapon ever known to have been used on Orinel was based upon the power of the rare element, carthagium, to annihilate the demetron, one of the many subatomic particles. It had been found (though where or when, he did not know) that the destruction of five demetrons per atom was the maximum which could be attained without dangerous by-effects. As this was sufficient to cause material decomposition, and as a certain amount of caution in regard to such things had become almost instinctive, carthagium was prepared in five-dem units only, the amount of a charge being calculated in the number of five-dems contained. It had been centuries since Orinel world polity had passed the stage of international conflict on a scale involving weapons producing such massive damage. No nation would now venture to use them, though all nations still ventured to make them. And everyone knew of the deadly, black, egg-shaped five-dem units of which each charge was composed. Apparently it had never occurred to anyone that the units were weapons in themselves. Apparently no nation possessing them had ever been obliged to arm overnight a people experienced in using no weapon but a rock or stone. It was only here and now in Tarnis that the two factors had met. A people deprived of anything more complex, lest they should turn on their oppressors, was now about to turn on their oppressors with something at the same time infinitely complex and equally simple.

And, Tonoro realized, gazing on the gaping structure and the settling dust with a sick feeling, the war with which this weapon would be chiefly waged had already begun.

CHAPTER TWELVE

Sarlamat faced the Conjoint Council—the five Chief Lords and the six Chief Guardians—and tried again to explain. "That is not the way the protective screen *works*!" he exclaimed. "It is not something solid, like a roof. It is not even something partially solid and partially vacant, like a net. Imagine a number of men scattered about a field. Someone throws a large ball at the field. At once, all the men rush towards the ball and put up their hands and catch it and try to prevent its touching the field. *That* is how the protective screen works —the particles are in suspension, they are sensitized; as soon as a body above a certain mass approaches, the particles rush together and interpose themselves between it and the area being—" He broke off, threw up his hands. Death approached on all sides, and he was here, lecturing like a pedagogue with all the time in the world.

"But they do *not* interpose themselves," Lord Losacamant objected. "We see it ourselves—these damned and devilish *gorum*-rocks that the brutes have made just go right through your so-called protection screen. So—"

"You must get bombs!" Guardian Othofarinal cried.

"*Gorum, gorum*, it has nothing to do with *gorum*: they aren't magic and they aren't rocks," Sarlamat declared, with passion. "They are five-dem units and the reason that the screen particles do not keep them out is because no one ever thought it would be necessary to make it possible for objects of such small mass to be screened out. If there were only time, *time*— But there is not—"

"*Bombs!*"

The Guardian was obsessed with the word and concept. He had never seen bombs or been anywhere near where they were dropped; perhaps he thought of them, consciously or otherwise, as objects with a sense of discrimination, possessing the proper social prejudices. "What do you expect bombs to do?" Sarlamat demanded. "Where would you have them dropped? On the cities, where half of our people have fled? On the country estates? On all of them? A charge big enough to destroy a city—drop it on one house? Because perhaps a Volanth is hiding in it? Perhaps your daughter or your grandson is hiding in it!

"Over the centuries this whole planet has deliberately built up a system of using short-range weapons because of the known insanity of developing larger, longer-range ones. No one is going to use the only major weapon in existence now —if it's used in an intranational war, the next step might be to use it in an international war. The risk's too great. When we—when I and the Commercial Deputy—is there still no news of him?—learned that the Bahon were arming the Quasi we never dreamed that they were arming them with *this!*"

The Conjoint Council had not been entirely still while he was speaking and now that he had stopped it burst again into full cry. It was meeting at Yellowtrees, Mothiosant's country estate, not because it was his or because of its historical associations (there was no time now for sentimental gestures), but because in the suddenness of the outbreak and the uncoordinated movements to and fro, it had provided a convenient, temporary rallying-place. The fabric and furnishings of the mansion were still intact, the Pemathi houseboys still attended neatly and promptly as ever.

Otherwise, though, nothing was the same. The Council, for all its noise and gesticulation—now and then for a moment relapsing into the ornate formalities of familiar times, then falling into abrupt and momentary silence, then bursting forth again—the Council was still in a state of shock. Not since the almost legendary age of Lord Maddary had the Volanth broken out into war. Ah, the view had always been that the Volanth were always doing so, and on this basis the periodic levies had gone out to punish them. But this—this carrying of war out to the estates, the very towns and cities of the Tarnisi—this was different! This was in truth a war! And in acknowledging this, they, in effect, acknowledged that the rest was all a lie. The Volanth for a thousand years had not really made war upon the Tarnisi. *But they were doing it now.*

Losacamant said, "If the Lermencasi intend to help us at all, if we aren't to be wiped out, then at least they will send us the same things—not '*gorum*-rocks,' you call them something else?—but they have them, too? They'll supply us with them, too, I must hope? Because if they do not, my brother, why— By my blood! Then all who have the Seven Signs will perish!"

Sarlamat made a haggard and weary motion with his face. He spoke, he said words. But not the words he was thinking. The Lermencasi could not care less about the Seven Signs and those who had them. He had sent signals, yes; scores of them. The reaction was principally anger against himself and Mothiosant for allowing events to get out of control. Anger was followed by suspicion, suspicion by caution. And then all emotion vanished behind clouds of words, phrases, regrets. What the Lermencasi would send— if anything—he could not guess. Himself, he had abandoned hope, would have tried to make his own escape, but these officious fools had trapped him here, and he did not know if he could make himself free of them again, or what good it might do him if he could. So he huddled in his robes of redupon-red and let the day's events unreel and gallop before his sunken, troubled, despairing eyes.

The vanishing-away of the Quasi colony which huddled in its disorder beyond the green belt of park and trees protecting the town from its contamination—this should have served him as warning: just as the abrupt drying-up of a spring warns of earthquake, as the abnormal retreat of the sea warns of tidal wave: it should have. But he was preoccupied, and it did not. They had heard a rumor, they were panic-stricken; he thought no more of it than this. Too, there were reports that a number of floats were missing, but when (preoccupied again, only partially considering the matter) he'd asked about it, his clerks assured him that it was nothing. A minor irregularity, soon to be set right. Isolated incidents—now, looking back, they seemed like plain informations, thick and fast. The border warden who had half-crashed his float and struggled from it to babble of Volanth who had made his house disappear by stoning it with *gorum-*rocks. Surely he was mad . . . no more. Three tally clerks coming back from a routine trip to check stores at Compound Five, two in one float and the other in a second, why —what could one have made of their confused account (the two, that is) of the third one in his single craft being alongside of them one moment and the next moment it had blown up? An engine fault, nothing more. The hydrofoil reported aground and half-destroyed. The failure of Compound Six to reply when signaled. And so on, and so on. Each, at the time, had appeared to be unconnected with the other. And so the day had passed, and although anxious at not seeing Mothiosant and puzzled about confused reports from Rophas Town, Sarlamat had still been able to retire at night and even to sleep.

He had not slept long.

The Volanth had swept down from the Outlands, seemingly, in full force. They had swarmed out of the hills and forests, the brush country and the marshes, the river valleys and the plains, like some abnormal animal migration—like *par,* fleeing before a fire. Clearly, not all of them had come afoot. Certainly some of the attacks had been made by air. The Bahon—infinitely clever of the Bahon though it all was, still—how could they have known where and how to attack the floats, first? so that escape was rendered all but impossible? Well, it didn't matter, it was a minor mystery. Baho was the equal of Lermencas. It was the Volanth, the Volanth!

Each had come laden with sacks of skin or baskets of withes, but their burdens contained no common contents.

Their burdens had grown lighter as they proceeded onward. And then, apparently, had grown heavier again. A rock in the hands of a Volanth was in itself a deadly weapon. The wild men could hit a bird on the wing at an incredible space, strike down a running rat at an unbelievable distance. Since the days of *The Volanthani* it had of course been illegal for them to possess even a club or a spear, a bow or an arrow. But no one could legislate against a rock! which in any event might be dropped and lost as soon as a patrol appeared. Nature supplied them with these weapons at every hand, and in a thousand years a very high degree of skill indeed can be developed.

Out of the forest and out of the night they came. One black egg cast like a stone through the black night. One house destroyed. If by chance the sound of screams indicated survivors, throw another. If by much, much rarer chance, a fire-charge speaks and shines in the darkness, one black egg dashed at the point the sound and sight came from. Then, in the darkness, press on. Press on. For a thousand years is a long, long time . . . and so is the half a thousand years which went before them.

Sarlamat snapped back into the present. Othofarinal had spoken to him. With difficult courtesy, he asked the Guardian to speak again. Silvery hair all awry, the Tarnisi repeated, "These foreign toys, the ones just long and broad enough for a single man—surely something might be done with them, I must hope? It is reported that many of them are at the sport pavilion at the river. Myself, my brother's son— Oh. Oh. I do not know. They are foreign things. You know of such inventions. We do not. Can nothing be done?"

Slowly, slowly, the outlines of an idea took form in Sarlamat's mind. "It is my thought that something might be done. But before proceeding to the river, you will accompany me to the armory, I must hope." He said this. And he arose.

* * *

Tonoro walked slowly through the dust- and rubble-choked streets of Tarnis Town. Tarnis, Thias, Rophas, all of the jewel-like cities of Tarnis which he had visited, all were the same. They glittered no more, their towers lay in the dust, their gardens were choked with ashes. Now and then, from one side or another, an echoing *crump* was heard. Perhaps some survivor had unwisely shown himself, maddened by grief or fear or thirst. Perhaps a Volanth was merely enjoying the noise and the still-novel sight of the destruction produced so easily and quickly. From time to time he heard —and saw—evidence that the Volanth were enjoying themselves in other ways as well. Sometimes the unwise survivor was a woman. More than once he had seen the events of the levy re-enacted in reverse, with now the hairy man pursuing the smooth woman. And, as before, always, always, the man overtook the woman. Threw her on her back in the dust and spread her shaking legs and mounted her. . . .

In his heart, Tonoro knew that no memory or mention of outrage could justify any other outrage. He knew in his heart that he should interfere. But he did not. His heart could convey no command to hand or mouth, for his heart was frozen. Atoral was dead.

He wore, as all the Quasi wore—and all the Volanth, they imagining it to be a sort of insigna or badge; no one told them otherwise—a strip of cloth bound around his head. It was dangerous, it might be fatal to be without it. Those same Signs which the Quasi had once been so glad to possess, or so bitter and aggrieved at not possessing them, were now no defense, but a danger. He, Tonoro, Quasi son of a Quasi, who had in his childhood, not much beyond his infancy, been hunted by the Tarnisi because he was a Quasi—he, that same Tonoro, who had so eagerly and so unwittingly paid to have himself transformed into the immaculate semblance of a Tarnisi—he now wore a strip of rag, filthier than a Volanth's breechclout, bound around his once-proud head, lest the questing Volanth should now mistake him for a Tarnisi.

Atoral's body he had not seen. He thought it was better that he had not, that he could not. Cominthal, with the same impatience with which he had promised the Tulan's house immunity, had announced that it had been destroyed despite that promise. "He did not know. I am sorry. It was a most regrettable error. . . ."

And the Volanth himself, a "civilized" one, who had in his earlier life even been licensed to live among the Tarnisi for a period for some purpose or other, he, too, repeated, and with evidence of sincere sorrow, "I did not know. I am sowwy. It was a most wegwetable ewwo." Genuine sorrow showed on his bearded face. He was not naked, none of them were anymore (save when they chose to be, in sordid scenes), all of them without exception now wore Tarnisi clothes . . .

wore them with a proud air, and . . . curiously . . . wore them well. Tonoro noted this with an ice-bound detachment that alone saved him from the horror of the irony: his world was dead, and he made mental fashion notes.

He remembered her, placing her fingers so gently on his wrist so soon after their first meeting, remembered her lovely body, so rich in promise, moving so confidently through the cool waters of the lake. Remembered her body in his arms, her voice in his ears. She had asked so little of him and had given him so much. While she was alive he had at first enjoyed their present without thought or care for a future in which they might not be together. More recently, as events had quickened, then rushed, he had at last begun to consider it. Atoral anywhere than in Tarnis? Atoral, daughter of Tarnis, and—when all was said and done—daughter of Tarnis's almost instinctive social code, the lover of a Quasi? The *wife* of one? He had decided that it was better, his not being able to see her, dead. But he could not and would not, despite every known negative, take the glib and evil way of thinking it was better that she was dead.

At least, though, he could see to it that murder and massacre did not reign unchallenged. He had been unable to do this when the Volanth were victims, those events had come too swift, too soon, he had been swept up in them; too, he had not known all that there was to know, had seen only their guilt before it was swallowed up in the greater guilt of their oppressors. But at least he was now able to see to it that the pattern wasn't totally reproduced in reverse. He had set aside designated areas of the port as sanctuary. When first one and then another and then a third Lermencasi freighter had unwarily put down and immediately been taken, their cargo of floats and fire-charges unloaded and confiscated, he had been able to see that all Tarnisi who had surrendered were allowed to leave on the freighters. His plans hadn't gone unchallenged.

Opposition had not come principally from either Volanth or Quasi, but from Bishdar Shronk, the Bahon agent. Impassionedly. "All of them deserve death," he had all but roared. "Fifteen hundred years of crime requires it! And all of these, too," he growled, his gesture taking in the quaking freightermen, "they deserve it, too, for their complicity."

But Tonoro had held firm. And when one of the last of the refugees had gone aboard—an older woman, he could not remember her name, but he could remember that she had visited him once and invited him to visit her ("We are famous for our sunken gardens. . . . I have charming granddaughters. . . ." What had happened to those gardens, cultivated with immense care for centuries? More: What had happened to those granddaughters?)—when she turned from departure and asked him, in a voice gone far beyond either despair or accusation, a question not even rhetorical, "You see what the Bahon are. How could you have allowed yourself to work with them?"—

—He had answered only in the words of the ancient proverb "The enemy of my enemy is my friend."

It was ironic, perhaps, that the palatial offices of the Commercial Delegation had not been harmed. Headquarters had, accordingly, been set up there, and there it was that Tonoro returned after his tour of the ruined city. There was much to do—food to be gathered and distribution guaranteed, the wounded to be attended to, the dead to be buried—

Without his asking it or without anyone's asking him to, he was now a leader. The Volanth in their new clothes came to him and asked him questions.

"There are Tarnisi hidden in the caves in such-and-such a place, my mother's son. Men and women and children. It is too difficult to reach them with the *gorum*-eggs. You will have those of the part-blood who know how to handle floats take us up so that we can attack them, I must hope."

"No. When I was a child they tried to kill me. Enough children have been killed. That's not the way of civilization. I will take a Pemathi and give him a message offering them safe-conduct for surrender, and you will see that it is done."

"It will be done that way, then, I must hope, my brother's son."

Agreement was not always reached. The Bahon—how soon they arrived! They spoke to him of plans for reconstruction, complex and promising plans. But he found himself dozing over them. Guards were posted; he retired for the night to the soft couch in the guest room where visitors had in former times *(former times!)* been offered recreation, and fell into troubled dreams. Someone shook him. A Pemathi. Atén aDuc. How did he come to be here in Tarnis? How was it that the freighters were so near? He could hear their blasts, the building was shaking too.

"What?" he cried, on his feet.

"The river!" someone shouted. Not Atén aDuc. Atén a Duc was not here. The noise was something else, something else that he did not know. "The river is on fire! The river is blowing up!"

And so it was and so it was. From the roof of the Delegation building he watched it, coiling through the city like a blazing serpent. Again and again the air and the ground and the water trembled with the explosions. Masses of burning matter hurtled through the air, fell upon the ruins and rubble, set them soon on fire. In a quarter of an hour the whole of Tarnis Town was all ablaze, the night was brighter and hotter than the day had ever been. It was impossible to fight it, it was—in the state of wreckage—useless even to try. He ordered a retreat to the port, far enough from both river and town.

The city blazed all that night and all that next day. The Volanth, in accounting for the rains which finally extinguished it, said that "the heat had melted the clouds." But that came later. It was still pouring when reports came that the Tarnisi had, somehow, rallied, and were attacking.

The report was true. They had come out of the steaming ruins, preceded by floats, the floats vanishing into the concealing rain as the attackers proceeded slowly on foot. Many pockets of them must have contributed to their numbers, for the work of mopping up had scarcely begun. Warily, the two groups approached. The Tarnisi seemed to lack cohesion, organization. Part of them scattered, part retreated. Still the Volanth came on. The five-dem unit was by far the more potent weapon, but if the Tarnisi could push through a mass fire-charge before—

But that was not their plan. What the plan was came out of the rains again behind and above the insurgent forces, were not even seen until, diving down, they were almost upon them. It may have been instinct rather than fearful awareness which made so many of the Volanth break and run; Tarnisi in floats in time of war had never meant anything but death before. It did not mean anything different now. Nor did running gain escape. Not all, perhaps not even most, tried to get away. Those who stood their ground aimed and threw their five-dem units, the black eggs which brought them victory before. Not one single float escaped, and not one man in any of them but had realized it must be so. But the destruction of the floats was not caused by the dark ovoids alone. *That,* some did escape—and this must have been the hope behind the suicide attack. There on that waste ground between river, town, and port, the smell of smoke mingling with the smell of the wet earth, shouts and cries and confusion, rage and terror, before the dust of the destroyed floats could sink, sodden, to the ground, the others had crashed. Crashed upon and in the midst of their enemies. Laden with fuel and fire charges and with, seemingly, every bit of scrap metal the craft could bear without losing altitude, each craft in itself a deadlier weapon than any had ever been before: crashed in a holocaust of fire and steam and flying, rending, metal.

And then and only then the Tarnisi came charging. They had the advantage of both surprise and confusion for long enough to gain the ground. They slipped in their enemies' blood and they got up and came charging on, firing, firing, screaming, running. The rains became torrential. Tarnisi, Volanth, mud, water, fire, disintegration, Quasi, shouts, body locked with slippery body, hands clawing at throats, thumbs gouging at eyes, teeth seeking and clicking and sinking into flesh, fist, and foot and, at the last, sheer pressure of weight. It was the last battle, it was the re-enactment of every ancient and bloody prophecy and legend. It was Ragnarok and Waterloo and Armageddon.

And the rain beat down upon all alike, as though to emphasize the hostility of the universe itself.

* * *

Sarlamat's face stared back at him, look for look, no withdrawal, no begging, no change, no regret. It was clean from the rains; no drop of blood remained in the wound. Indeed, it seemed that no drop of blood remained in the body. Cominthal, standing by Tonoro's side, bent, and spat in the dead man's face. Tonoro said, "Why bother. . . ."

"He hated us until the last," his cousin said. "It was he who rallied the Tarnisi, wasn't it? It was his idea to pour the fuel into the river and then to fasten the fire-charges onto those foreign water-things of yours and turn them loose to burn the river and the town. And it was his idea, too—that last, mad try with the floats. He almost won. He hated us."

"No," Tonoro said, wearily. "He didn't. He didn't hate us at all. He wasn't a Tarnisi, he was—probably—a Lermencasi, disguised, as I was. He had no prejudice, believe me. He didn't hate us. He was indifferent to us."

Cominthal said, "Then that makes it worse. I can find it

in my heart to understand the Tarnisi. They did what their fathers did. He didn't have that excuse."

Tonoro nodded. He felt drained of hatred, drained of love, fear, ambition, desire. It was as well that he did not even have the desire to rest, because there was no time to rest. To the Pemathi standing behind him, he said, gesturing, "Bury him. Bury them all."

To Cominthal he said, "We have to talk about the future."

The man nodded, frowned. "The Bahon have many plans. . . ."

They did, indeed. And, indeed, it was about those plans that Tonoro had to talk. After the battle the victors had bewailed their dead. And after bewailing and then burying, a great silence seemed to descend upon the land. Here and there, surprisingly, fire still smoldered. Now and then a dazed or a terrified Tarnisi survivor still turned up. No one seemed to know what to do. No one knew, exactly, what he even wanted to do. Except, of course, the Bahon.

Bishdar Shronk, growling now in a different key, said, "Wandering around and sight-seeing will accomplish no good. Looting and parading in fancy clothes will accomplish no good. Nor will returning to the Outlands and trying to take up the old ways. It is necessary to begin the work of reconstruction immediately, before these useless practices become habitual. Only by proceeding according to the plans of the United Syndicates can the work of reconstruction be accomplished successfully."

The weight of truth and experience was behind his words. A power vacuum existed, and it had to be filled. One way or the other. Tonoro agreed. Cominthal agreed. The Quasi could no longer live as strivers or as parasites. The Volanth could not return to hunting, fishing and primitive farming, as though nothing had changed but the disappearance of the oppressor class. The tenuous screen of Tarnisi obscurantism was no longer there to keep out the present century. The law of social gravity would now work unchecked; the present *had* to come in. If no nation, no modern nation, presided over its entrance, then private people, even, no doubt, pirates and freebooters, would provide their own presence. Logically, the Bahon were best suited to the work. They were experienced in it. They were desirous of doing it. And, perhaps most of all, they were there on hand. They were present.

So, then, the Bahon. And their plans.

Compulsory education. Voluntary ignorance was a luxury the new nation could not afford.

Compulsory personal engagement in the work of construction and reconstruction. Voluntary idleness was a vice the new nation could not afford.

Compulsory commitment to the most modern forms of syndicated agriculture and industry. Individualism was a crime the new nation could not afford.

Books, plans, scrolls, screened illustrations, speeches, exhortations, diagrams, showing how the Bahon would guide, how the Bahon would build, the Bahon create, the Bahon market, the Bahon assist, do, teach, advance, improve—

Tonoro blinked. He nodded, almost out of habit. He frowned, very slightly. In the clear air, still smelling of the smoke which was no longer visible except in a very few places, down the road which had been partially cleared, a crew of Pemathi were at work bringing up supplies out of the unburned ruins. It was rather surprising how much still remained. "What are they doing with them?" he asked.

Bishdar Shronk said, in his rough, confident voice, "They work for mercenary wages as part of the system of exploitation. So it is only fair that, for the present, they work without wages as part of the system of reconstruction. In a very short while the program of education will be extended to them as well, for—"

"Yes, yes. But what are they *doing* with those goods? Now that I think of it, I observed that Pemathi crews are at work in all the warehouses. What's up?"

Bishdar Shronk nodded his assent to the serious validity of the question. "The people of Bahon," he explained, "have made innumerable sacrifices over a long period of time, building up a free system to the point where they are now, fortunately, able—and not only able, but willing and happy— to have aided and to aid other peoples and nations in the task of doing the same. By partial, I must emphasize, only partial compensation, your people will demonstrate their willingness to sacrifice something in order to build and to prove to all the other oppressing and exploiting nations that. . . ." He spoke for a very long time, fluently, persuasively, coherently. And all the time he was talking, the supplies continued to be put in readiness to be sent off to Baho.

He was so astonished at their not going off that he could scarcely express his outrage that he and the other Bahon were going off, instead. Finally, his growling done, his large mouth small and grim, he spoke shortly. "We will be back," he said. "We cannot be kept out."

"You will, indeed, I must hope," Tonoro agreed. "And not in anger, either. But on terms which will be mutually agreeable. And not alone."

Cominthal was half-glad, half-doubtful. "Their plans were too difficult," he said. "They wanted to move too fast. We aren't used to that. But . . . What are we going to do?" he asked. "Now? Instead. . . ."

Tonoro explained his own notions to him. Presently, he would explain them to all the others, Quasi and Volanth and prisoners and refugees alike. Tarnis was part of Orinel. And all of Orinel had now to help them here in Tarnis, those nations which belonged to the Interleague Council and those which did not. Everyone could contribute something. Everyone would. Even the Bahon.

"Even the Lermencasi?"

"Even the Lermencasi."

Cominthal sucked in his breath as though he found it a trifle painful. Still, he seemed relieved. Still, he seemed puzzled.

"But . . . you said . . . prisoners and refugees, too. Why?"

"When I said, 'everyone,' I meant, 'everyone.' Even the Tarnisi. Oh, yes. Oh, yes. Even the Tarnisi. The sins of this generation of them were heavy and great. But they have paid greatly and heavily. The debt of this generation has been paid, and to hold any generation to blame for the debts or the deeds of another generation is insane.

"We need help. The Bahon can teach us industry, the Lermencasi can teach us commerce, the Pemathi can teach us diligence, and so on and on. But who will teach us how to live when we are not being taught? We cannot learn and build and buy and sell all the time. I see so clearly now that we will learn these other matters from those who are really, despite everything, closest to us of all. Some, of course, won't want to. Either they will fight on and be killed and captured and sent away, or they can go away of their own free will. And those who are already in exile, they can make their choice: Return and work with us, or stay where you are. 'You forgive us and we will forgive you.' Or else, wander in exile and warm yourselves with your hate.

"It may be easier for the Volanth. They endured violence, they performed violence. The slate is clean. But for you . . . for the Quasi . . . it may be more difficult. We were closer to the Tarnisi; they spurned us more often simply because we were—and are—closer. Can we lie to ourselves, deny our own biology? We are at least as much them as we are anything else. It wasn't just imitating, trying to pass. It was acting out a realized truth. And now all of that must move into a newer, better phase."

Cominthal gave a long, deep sigh. "It never was easy. Maybe we just exchange the hard things, this one for that one. But, average them all, it should come out easier. Well, you talk first. We'll ask them to come and listen.—Where?"

Fortunately or unfortunately, the Tree of Consultation was still standing. Its trunk was broad, its branches wide, and it stood between the sunlight and the shade.